The Sound
of Freedom

• KATHY KACER •

 annick press
toronto + berkeley

Cover art by Félix Girard
Cover design by Kong Njo
Edited by Barbara Berson
Designed by Kong Njo

Annick Press Ltd.

We acknowledge the support of the Canada Council for the Arts and the Ontario Arts Council, and the participation of the Government of Canada/ la participation du gouvernement du Canada for our publishing activities.

ONTARIO ARTS COUNCIL
CONSEIL DES ARTS DE L'ONTARIO
an Ontario government agency
un organisme du gouvernement de l'Ontario

Cataloging in Publication

Kacer, Kathy, 1954-, author
   The sound of freedom / Kathy Kacer.

Issued in print and electronic formats.

ISBN 978-1-55451-970-5 (hardcover).–ISBN 978-1-55451-969-9 (softcover).–
ISBN 978-1-55451-972-9 (PDF).–ISBN 978-1-55451-971-2 (EPUB)

   I. Title.

PS8571.A33S68 2017   jC813'.54   C2017-905812-6
                                                  C2017-905813-4

Published in the U.S.A. by Annick Press (U.S.) Ltd.
Distributed in Canada by University of Toronto Press.
Distributed in the U.S.A. by Publishers Group West.

Printed in Canada

Visit us at: www.annickpress.com
Visit Kathy Kacer at kathykacer.com

Also available in e-book format. Please visit www.annickpress.com/ ebooks.html for more details.

MIX
Paper from
responsible sources
FSC® C004071

To Maya and Elisheva –
a new generation.
And for Gabi and Jake –
with love as always.

—K.K.

"There are two possibilities for me:
To win through with all my plans, or to fail.
If I win, I shall be one of the greatest men in history.
If I fail, I shall be condemned and despised."

—ADOLF HITLER[1]

"One has to build a fist against anti-Semitism.
A first class orchestra will be this fist."

—BRONISLAW HUBERMAN[2]

"Last one to the bakery has to pay," shouted Anna, bolting down the street.

"Wait, you didn't warn me," her friend Renata yelled before dashing after her.

The two girls raced, pigtails flying, through the streets of Krakow, on their way home from school. Anna thought she was comfortably in the lead until she glanced over her shoulder and realized that Renata was right on her heels. At the last second, Renata sprinted ahead of her and rounded the corner, coming to a stop in front of Mrs. Benna's bakery shop.

"Not fair," Anna said a moment later as she pulled up. She was panting heavily, and even though the air was cold and the wind was biting, she could feel the sweat rolling down her back under her heavy jacket.

"What do you mean, not fair?" Renata replied. Her cheeks were flushed from the run. "It was your idea. And I'll have my donut filled with chocolate, please."

Anna raised her arms in defeat and entered the bakery with Renata. They quickly found a table and ordered their sweets.

Stopping at Mrs. Benna's shop on the way home from school was a Tuesday afternoon tradition for the two girls. Tuesdays were when Anna's father gave music lessons at their house. He was a gifted clarinetist who played in the famous Krakow Philharmonic Orchestra and lectured at the music academy. Many families in town lined up to send their children to learn to play clarinet from Anna's father, the renowned Avrum Hirsch. So on Tuesdays, Anna had permission to stay out after school with Renata—that is, as long as the two of them also got some homework done.

"You have icing sugar all over your face," Anna said after she and Renata had polished off their treats.

"Do I?" Renata reached up to brush the sugar and crumbs away. "It's so good. I could eat donuts filled with chocolate all day long."

"Agreed! Except that I'll take mine filled with strawberry preserves."

At that, Renata made a face. "Nothing is better than chocolate."

Anna pushed her plate aside and pulled out her notebook. Mrs. Benna never minded when the girls came to her shop after school. "You set a good example for other young people who walk in here," the shopkeeper said. As long as no one was lining up for their table, Mrs. Benna said they could stay as long as they wanted.

Anna flipped through the pages of her math assignment and chewed on the end of her pencil. "I don't know how I'd get through math without you," she said, looking up at Renata.

"You're just as smart as I am," Renata replied. "Just in different subjects. I'm better with numbers, but you're the one who helps me with literature."

Anna and Renata had been great friends for years, ever since they started school, spotting each other across the classroom and exchanging smiles. They met each weekday morning at Anna's corner to walk together to school. Now, at age twelve, they were as close as sisters. Baba, Anna's grandmother, always said they could have been twins with their jet-black curly hair and dark eyes. But when it came to their studies, they were as different as they could possibly be. Anna loved to read while Renata could untangle a math equation faster than anyone in the class. Anna loved art while Renata always claimed she had ten thumbs when it came to drawing or painting. Anna loved music, and even though Renata took clarinet lessons from Anna's father, she hated to practice. Anna always reasoned that the differences between them were what made them great friends—complements of each other and a perfect team. One couldn't manage without the other to help. Today was no exception. The girls finished off their homework in record time.

"Will you come over to my place?" Anna asked as they began to pack up their books. "Baba is making her famous beef stew."

"Sounds delicious!"

"And maybe she'll give us a cooking lesson." Anna's grandmother loved to cook.

Renata nodded. "Sure. My mother will be thrilled that I'm learning. She can barely make a cup of tea."

"It can't be that bad!"

"Trust me, it is. Last week, she burnt the chicken and served rice that was still as hard as gravel. I need all the help I can get."

"I'm sure Baba will be happy to include you. And then, when we're done, you can help me find a dress to wear to that concert that my father is playing in." That was another difference between the two girls. Renata loved to dress up while Anna didn't give a thought to fashion and "girly" things. Baba was the one who always insisted that she wind hair ribbons around her long pigtails, or wear fancy dresses. Anna found all of that so tiresome.

"You can borrow my scarf," Renata said, tugging at the bright green silk that stood out against her shiny coal-black eyes. "It'll be perfect with just about anything in your closet."

Just then, the bell above the door to the bakery shop rang and a group of boys entered. Anna recognized them from school, though she didn't have much to do with them. They were older and a couple of grades ahead. And they usually kept to themselves— that is, unless they were going after the weaker kids at school. They had that nasty reputation. Lately, they seemed to be targeting Jewish kids. Another boy from their school had been chased home by one of these boys. Everyone was talking about it. The bully threw rocks at the younger boy and shouted terrible insults. Anna and Renata looked at each other nervously. Both of them were Jewish, and they knew that it was better to stay away from these boys.

The boys were jostling one another and talking loudly. One pounded his fist on the counter and demanded, "Hey, we need some service."

Mrs. Benna approached from the other side of the shop. Her eyes flashed and her mouth narrowed

into a thin line. "There will be none of that in my res-
taurant," she said sternly. "If you don't show better
manners, then I want you out of here."

The boy who had banged on the counter took
a step toward Mrs. Benna. He was just about to say
something when one of his friends grabbed him by
the arm. "Come on. Let's find somewhere else to go.
This isn't worth it."

And with that, the boys turned and left. Anna exhaled a long, deep breath and shuddered.

"Those boys give me the creeps," Renata said.

Anna nodded, a knot settling in the pit of her
stomach. And it wasn't just the boys that made her
nervous. They were simply a reminder of the other
troubles that seemed to be descending on her city
of Krakow and across all of Poland. Lately, she had
heard stories of Jewish people being attacked on the
streets, pushed off the sidewalk and made to walk in
the gutter, or forced to pick up garbage. At first, the
victims were the most observant Jewish men, those
with long beards, full-length coats, and bowler hats.
They stood out and were easily targeted. But more re-
cently, the violence had spread to the general Jewish
community—people not unlike Anna and Renata.

Her baba had said that everything changed when
Adolf Hitler came to power in Germany. She called him
a maniac and said he'd made everyone feel unsafe.

"My parents have been talking a lot about what's happening to Jewish families," Renata was saying. "The attacks, the name calling. They're afraid those things are only the beginning."

"The beginning of what?" Anna put her coat on and grabbed her bag of books.

Renata shook her head.

"I don't think anything worse is going to happen," Anna continued, although what her friend said was making her even more anxious now. And it didn't help that when they were thanking Mrs. Benna and saying good-bye, the shopkeeper leaned closer and said, "I'd stay away from those boys if I were you. One at a time, they're a nuisance. But a group of them ..."

She didn't finish the sentence. And Anna didn't want to hear any more. She linked her arm in Renata's and pulled her out of the bakery shop. Outside, Anna flipped her thick-braided pigtails off her shoulders, pulled her knitted cap down on her head, and lifted the collar of her coat up around her ears. She needed to steer the conversation to a better place. "My father might still be teaching when we get to my house. So we'll have to be really quiet until his student leaves."

Renata remained silent.

"Are you okay?" Anna asked, turning to look at her friend.

Renata still looked troubled. "Those boys …"

"Don't be afraid of them, Renata," Anna said, mustering more certainty than she was feeling. The girls were passing through the Jewish quarter of Krakow, where the streets pulsed with activity. This was familiar territory: the old synagogue Anna and her family attended for the high holidays on her right, restaurants that overflowed with patrons up ahead, and the market where Baba bought fruit and vegetables just around the corner.

"It's just that my parents keep listening to the news reports from other countries," Renata continued. "And the news isn't good. Even Mrs. Benna warned us to be careful."

"She just meant those boys. And we will."

"I suppose you're right," Renata replied. Then she shook her head as if she were trying to clear any nasty thoughts away. "I hope your grandmother has a couple of extra aprons. I like to make a mess when I cook."

Anna laughed and the two girls continued to wind their way home. Nothing terrible had happened, Anna thought, allowing herself to relax. And soon, she and Renata would be home and cooking with Baba. That was the last thought she had before she suddenly saw them again.

CHAPTER 2

Anna yanked Renata's arm closer and pulled her to an abrupt stop. "Look!" She pointed ahead.

The boys from the bakery were emerging from Mr. Kaplansky's butcher shop, the place where Baba shopped for their meat. The butcher was a sweet man with a kind smile who had always had a candy for Anna when she accompanied her grandmother to his store. The boys were laughing and shoving one another. "You stay right there, old man," one of them called over his shoulder. "We're just going to do a little redecorating out here."

The anxiety Anna had felt earlier suddenly swelled once more. Something told her that they couldn't get in the middle of whatever was happening up ahead. Perhaps if they didn't move, they wouldn't be seen. She gripped Renata's arm more tightly.

One of the boys carried a small tin in one hand. In the other hand, he held a paintbrush. Had he been holding those things when they were in Mrs. Benna's store? Anna couldn't remember. While the boy's friends stood and watched, he dipped the brush in the tin and began to paint on the large window in front of Mr. Kaplansky's store. He painted big, black strokes—up, down, and across, while his friends egged him on. A moment later, he stood back. There on the store window was a giant Star of David. "Don't stop!" another boy demanded. "Finish it off!"

Anna and Renata remained glued to their spot. Behind her collar, Anna's face had grown hot. Suddenly, she spied Mr. Kaplansky staring at the boys from his doorway. His eyes were dark and angry. One of the boys spotted him and shouted, "Hey, we told you to stay inside." The butcher quickly ducked back into his shop.

Anna glanced around. *Why doesn't someone do something?* she wondered desperately. The street had become strangely quiet, and those few people who were out hurried by, burying their faces into their jackets and scarves.

Just then, Anna spotted Constable Zabek, the police chief, approaching from around the corner. His daughter Sabina also attended Anna's school. *Finally!* Anna breathed a sigh of relief. Help had arrived. Constable Zabek was a portly man, and the front of his uniform was pulled tight across his round belly, the buttons threatening to pop. The police chief strolled over to Mr. Kaplansky's store and took a long look at the scene in front of him. But instead of doing anything, instead of shouting at the boys to stop, or driving them off, or even arresting them, the police chief simply stood next to Mr. Kaplansky's shop with his hands clasped behind his back. He had a small smile on his face and watched everything that was happening with a detached kind of curiosity, as if he were watching a crowd of children in the playground.

The boys continued to jeer. "Finish it. *Finish it.* FINISH IT!" Each chant grew louder than the one before. And as they repeated this refrain, the boy with the paint can dipped his brush once more and then painted a slow, thick X through the Star of David. His message was clear. Jews were not wanted here.

Constable Zabek looked over at Anna and Renata, who were still frozen. He pulled himself to his fullest height. "You're not here to look at the view," he bellowed. "Move on!"

That was all it took. Anna and Renata grabbed hands, and together they ran. It was only when they reached the corner, close to their houses, that Renata pulled free and faced Anna.

"I'm going home," she said.

"But I thought you were coming over."

"Not now. I can't. I need to go home. I'm sorry, Anna."

And with that, Renata took off in the opposite direction. Anna felt another chill surround her as she turned and headed for home.

Once inside her house, Anna paused to catch her breath and to listen for whatever sound might greet her. A clarinet played softly in the background. Papa was still giving lessons. She would have to wait before talking to him about what had just happened. She hung up her coat and held her cold hands up to her cheeks, feeling the heat that was still there, a combination of lingering fear and the flush of having sprinted home. Then she ducked into the kitchen where Baba was making dinner, adding chopped onions and spices to a bowl with chunks of meat in it and mixing the concoction together with a big wooden spoon.

Anna kissed her grandmother on the cheek, and Baba raised her eyebrows as if to ask how her day had been. Anna nodded and gave her grandmother a weak smile. There would be no cooking lesson with Renata today. And she knew she couldn't say a word to her grandmother about the incident on the street, at least not yet. Baba would be reluctant to let Anna out of her sight if she thought her granddaughter was in any danger. Anna couldn't frighten Baba, who worried too much about everything as it was.

Baba had come to live here after Anna's mother passed away a year earlier. She'd had a sudden fever that went higher and higher until she looked as if she were on fire. And then everything in her mother's body had just stopped. The doctor said an infection had weakened her. She was gone in a matter of weeks. Baba said that her body had turned off, like turning off a lamp. But that did not make sense to Anna. You could turn a lamp back on.

When Baba moved in, she had taken the sad, sick smell of death from the house and filled it with the sweet aroma of cinnamon and vanilla and chocolate. Baba's cooking had brought life back into their home. Having her there was like being wrapped in a warm blanket all the time. "Her heart is as big as this house," Papa always said. Anna believed that Baba's heart was even bigger than that.

Anna pulled a bowl from the cupboard and reached for a sharp knife to shred some cabbage for dinner. Just then, the unmistakable squeak of a clarinet from

Papa's student drifted in from the other room. She recognized instantly who was playing. Today, it was her friend Stefan Ungar. Not all of Papa's students played as beautifully as her father would have liked. Stefan sounded like a sheep. And listening to Renata play was like listening to a howling dog. Of course, Anna had never said that to either of their faces! But she couldn't help the way she felt about their musical ability. And they weren't the only ones. Some of Papa's other students sounded like barnyard animals as well. Some sounded like geese or ducks.

But then there were the ones who played beautifully. Anna sighed as she thought about Sabina Zabek. Even though she was confused and disturbed that Constable Zabek had just ignored the boys who vandalized Mr. Kaplansky's store, Anna had to admit that she could listen to Sabina play forever. Her notes hung in the air like stars in the sky. Sometimes, when Anna heard her play, it was like listening to sunshine.

Anna finished making the cabbage salad and carried the bowl into the dining room. As she set it on the table, Stefan hit a note that sent a shudder up and down her spine. Anna rolled her eyes. At that very moment, she caught her father's eye.

Later, when Stefan had left and they were sitting down to dinner, Papa turned to her.

"Do not be unkind to my students," he said, seriously. "They are doing their best." He took off his glasses as he spoke, which was always a sign that he meant business.

Anna opened her mouth to say something and then stopped. She didn't mean to be cruel. But she knew what good music sounded like. When Papa played the clarinet, he could make the instrument sound as gentle as falling rain, as spooky as a dark night, or as mellow as a cup of tea. He had taught Anna to play as well, and it was something that had brought the two of them closer together, especially after her mother died. Some of the light had gone out of Papa then as well. When Anna played, she tried not to sound like one of the barnyard animals!

"Everyone learns to play at their own pace," Papa continued. "Not every student is as gifted as Sabina Zabek."

At that, Anna's eyes flared. *Sabina's father is a horrible man who did nothing about those bullies!* That's what she wanted to say, but instead, she pursed her lips together. Now was not the time to talk, not with Baba sitting right there with the two of them.

"Perhaps later this evening, you and I can practice together, Annichka," Papa continued. "You can show me how much better you are than your friend Stefan Ungar." Anna smiled and lowered her eyes. She knew that when Papa referred to her with this term of endearment, all was well.

Anna pushed her spoon absentmindedly around the soup bowl.

"Don't you like my *krupnik*, Anna?" Baba asked, pointing to the barley soup that was thick with carrots, potatoes, and other vegetables. "You're not eating. Are you sick?" Nothing made Baba happier than feeding her family, and nothing registered more concern than if Anna or Papa weren't eating.

"It's too much for me, Baba. But it's probably the best soup you've ever made." Anna added this last part to make her grandmother smile.

"Yes," Baba said, grinning from ear to ear. "I added some extra parsley this time. I think it was just what the soup needed. Sit, sit," she added as Anna jumped up to clear the table. "I'll bring the meat in. You stay here and talk with your father."

"Tell me how school was, Annichka," Papa asked as soon as Baba had left the dining room. It was the opportunity that Anna had been waiting for.

"I need to tell you what happened today," Anna began, lowering her voice to make sure Baba did not hear. She quickly told her father about Mr. Kaplansky's store and the boys who had painted the star on his window. She told him that Renata's parents were worried about the things that were happening to Jews in Krakow. Finally, she told him about the police chief, Sabina's father, who did nothing to stop the thugs. "He was acting as if he thought what they were doing was okay—as if he wanted them to keep going!"

Papa sighed heavily. "Poor Mr. Kaplansky," he said. "I'll go by his shop tomorrow and see how he's doing." Then he frowned. "Those boys didn't try to do anything to you, did they?"

Anna shook her head.

"Good. Just make sure you stay away from them. They sound as if they are nothing but trouble!"

Papa sounded just like Mrs. Benna. "But what about Constable Zabek," Anna cried. "I don't understand why he would allow them to do that!"

Just then, Baba returned to the dining room carrying a platter of stew and vegetables. Anna sank back in her seat, frustrated that Papa had not answered that last question, as if he hadn't even heard it. And he hadn't said anything about Renata's parents, either. But the opportunity to ask her father anything more was gone, and the rest of the meal passed with small talk.

When they were finished eating and Anna had helped clear the table, they gathered around the radio in the sitting room. There was a concert that Papa wanted to listen to featuring a world-famous violinist named Bronislaw Huberman. He was going to be playing a violin concerto by the Russian composer Tchaikovsky, one of Papa's favorites. Papa turned on the radio and it sputtered to life. Although Anna was still itching to continue the conversation with her father about what had happened that day, for now, she settled in a soft chair and laid her head back.

Anna had been listening to music her whole life. "From before you were born," Baba often joked. Music was like medicine for Anna. It stirred her heart, made her laugh, and at times brought on the tears. This evening, she knew that the music would help calm her, and then, later, when she was getting ready for bed, perhaps that would be the time when she could speak to her father privately. He would let her know that the incident with the police chief was a chance occurrence. He would tell her that she didn't have to worry and that they were not in any kind of danger. He would say things like, "Relax, Annichka. There is nothing to fear." And her mind would be eased. Yes, after the concert would be the perfect time to talk to Papa.

The wistful sound of the violin filled the sitting room. "Listen to the tone of Huberman's violin, Anna," said Papa. He loved to add his commentary when a concert was being played. "He's so expressive. I once had an opportunity to hear him perform when he gave a concert here in Krakow, though that was many years ago." Papa smiled, lost in his own story. "You know, he began to play when he was only eight years old. He was known as a young Jewish prodigy —a genius! Years of practice, that's what it takes."

Suddenly, the radio crackled with static and the music stopped right in the middle of a passage. A moment later, a man's voice came on the air to announce that the concert was being interrupted for an important news report.

"What now?" Papa asked, standing up and moving over to the radio.

The unmistakable voice of Adolf Hitler filled the sitting room. Anna sat up in her seat. It was not often that she heard the leader of Germany address the nation. Usually, Papa would change the station when one of Hitler's speeches was on the air. But for some reason, this time Papa's hand just hovered over the dial.

Anna already knew a lot about what was happening in Germany under Hitler's rule. You couldn't live in Krakow in 1935 and not know these things. The newspapers were full of stories about the events in Europe. Besides, Renata often told her about the political news that she learned from her parents, who seemed to talk a lot about those things.

Under Adolf Hitler and his Nazi party, there were new laws in Germany designed to single out Jewish people and stop them from owning land and getting jobs. These laws included ways to pick out Jews by examining their noses, ears, and hair. Anna wondered what difference it made if her nose was longer than some others or if her hair was thicker, darker, and curlier. That had nothing to do with the person she was inside. Hitler was proclaiming that by identifying Jews and separating them from everyone else, he was protecting the honor of German citizens. But Anna couldn't understand why Jewish people were such a threat to that honor. What threat was poor Mr. Kaplansky? It was hard to imagine those new laws in Germany. And Germany was right next door to Poland! Would those same laws come to her country next?

Anna turned her attention back to the radio. Hitler was talking about how he was building the German army to be strong and unbeatable—to be able to defend itself against any who would act against it. He talked about providing jobs and creating good schools for all German citizens. He talked about all the things that would make Germany the strongest country in the world. A Polish journalist was translating the speech as it was being spoken. But in the background, Anna could hear Hitler's voice. It sounded as if he were spitting the words out of his mouth. After nearly every sentence, Anna could hear crowds of people cheering and chanting his name.

Papa seemed frozen as he stood over the radio. Baba sat with her head buried in her hands. But Anna distinctly heard her utter the word *maniac* under her breath. Anna looked from her father to her grandmother. The same sick feeling was rising once again in her stomach. And even though Hitler hadn't said anything about Jewish families, somehow Anna knew that this speech and the incident she had witnessed earlier in the day were linked. And then, just as she thought the speech might be ending, Hitler launched into a final rant about getting rid of all those who might threaten the future of his nation. One statement leapt out at her.

"First, we will cleanse Germany of all Jews. Country after country will follow."

Papa switched the radio off with a quick turn of the dial. At first, no one spoke. Then he slowly straightened and turned to face his daughter.

"Well, I guess the concert will be over now," he began. His voice was quivering like it did when he was upset. "Annichka, go and get ready for bed."

"But, what does—"

"Please don't ask me anything," Papa interrupted. He removed his glasses and rubbed his eyes. "It's late. You need to go to sleep."

The tone in Papa's voice was clear. Anna rose from her chair and went to give her grandmother a kiss. Baba barely moved from her hunched-over position. When Anna walked by her father, he grabbed her in a tight hug and held her for a long time. It did little to ease her growing fear. There would be no more discussion with Papa tonight, no reassurances. She was left with even more questions about their safety than before.

CHAPTER
4

Anna barely slept that night. Every time she closed her eyes, her mind was filled with dark images of Mr. Kaplansky's store being vandalized and the police chief shouting at her to move away. And in the background, the angry voice of Adolf Hitler was ranting that all Jews would be driven from the country. Anna would bolt awake, sweating and panting. And when she laid her head down again and closed her eyes, the whole nightmare would repeat. Light was beginning to drift in from below her window blinds when she finally dropped off into an exhausted sleep. And then it felt as if only minutes had passed before Papa was knocking on her door, telling her it was time to get up and get ready for school. Her head felt as heavy as the snow that fell in Krakow in the deep winter.

As hard as it was to get up, Anna was relieved to get out of the house. Perhaps the fresh air would clear her mind. And more than anything, she needed to talk to Renata. Her friend had run off, and Anna was worried about her—worried for both of them. Renata was waiting for her on the corner as she did most mornings. Anna raised her arm to wave to her friend and then stopped. Even from a distance, she could see the dark circles around Renata's eyes.

"You look terrible," Anna blurted out when she reached the corner.

"I couldn't sleep at all."

"Neither could I. Did you tell your parents what happened?"

Renata nodded. "They're even more worried than they were before. What about you?"

Anna sighed. "My father looks worried but he won't really talk to me about anything. We heard one of Adolf Hitler's speeches on the radio." She filled Renata in on Hitler's rant about ridding the country of Jews.

"My parents have the radio on all the time," Renata replied. "I can't listen to those speeches anymore."

The girls were approaching the center of town and Mr. Kaplansky's store. Anna wanted to stare straight ahead and not look over at the store window. She could try to pretend that nothing was any different from any other morning when she walked this way. But she knew that was not the case. As she glanced over at the store, there it was: the big black star with the thick X painted over it. A shiver as sharp as electricity passed through Anna's body. Mr. Kaplansky was nowhere to be seen and Anna wasn't even sure what she would have said to him if he had been there.

She could feel Renata stiffen beside her. When Anna turned back to look at her, her face was as white as the moon on a clear night. "I know what you're thinking," Anna said, trying to reassure her friend, "and I feel it too. But I'm sure Mr. Kaplansky is okay. And there's nothing we could have done for him. I'm sure of that."

"You're right," Renata replied. "I don't know what would have happened if those boys had turned on us."

"We need to stop being scared. Or at least try to stop thinking about all of this." Anna realized that she sounded feeble. Perhaps she was trying to convince herself as much as Renata.

"It's not just Mr. Kaplansky," Renata said.

What more is there?

"I-I want to t-tell you something."

Why was Renata stuttering?

"But I can't talk too much about it. I want to, but I can't."

And what was she hiding? "You know you can trust me to keep a secret. You can tell me anything." Renata was usually so chatty, and bright as a light bulb. The incident with Mr. Kaplansky had scared Anna, too, but Renata was walking and talking as if the light had gone out of her.

"I know. It's just ..."

"Just what?"

They were arriving at school. Up ahead, Anna could see her classmates gathering in front of the school building. Stefan was there, waving to both of them.

Renata sighed deeply. "I'll tell you when I can. Soon. Just not now. Please don't say anything to Stefan."

Stefan strode across the field and came to a stop in front of Anna and Renata. "Did you hear me play yesterday?" he asked, looking directly at Anna. "I'm sounding like a professional musician, don't you think?" Stefan always had the kind of impish grin on his face that made you wonder if he was joking with you. But this time, Anna knew that he was dead serious.

In spite of her troubling conversation with Renata, Anna had to stifle a smile. She was tempted to call him Stefan the sheep right to his face. But she remembered what her father had said about not being unkind. "You're getting ... much better, Stefan," she replied, choosing her words carefully. "Practice makes perfect."

Stefan nodded. "That's what your father says all the time." Then he turned to Renata. "Good," he said. "I'm glad you're here. I was working on these math problems most of last night." He fumbled in his schoolbag to find his homework. "I just need to check a few of these answers with you before we go inside." He extended his notebook toward Renata. But she did not take it. And her head was hanging so low on her chest that Anna could not even see her eyes.

Stefan looked puzzled. "Are you okay?" he asked, still holding his notebook out in front of him.

Anna knew that Renata's gloom had everything to do with the vandalism of Mr. Kaplansky's store along with whatever secret she was hiding. But Anna also knew that she couldn't ask about that. She had promised not to.

"Did you hear about what happened at Mr. Kaplansky's store?" Stefan suddenly asked. It was as if he had been reading her mind. "Those boys in the upper grades are getting worse than ever."

"It's not just the boys," Anna replied.

"What are you talking about?" asked Stefan. Renata looked up, her eyes dancing nervously from Stefan to Anna and back again.

But Anna did not have a chance to respond. Over Stefan's shoulder, she could see Sabina Zabek approaching from across the schoolyard.

Anna was not close to the police chief's daughter, but Sabina came to her house for clarinet lessons, so they usually greeted each other pleasantly enough. And Renata often helped Sabina with math problems. But today, following closely on Sabina's heels, were a couple of the same boys who had painted the star on Mr. Kaplansky's store. They flanked her like guards at the president's palace. Sabina came to a full stop right in front of Anna.

"Hello, Sabina," said Anna eyeing her two bodyguards.

Sabina folded her arms across her body and stared at Anna. "You know, it won't be long before you're not going to be allowed to come to this school anymore, or any school, for that matter."

"Excuse me?" Anna was stunned by Sabina's declaration.

"My father says it can't come soon enough." The boys behind her laughed and nudged one another.

Anna narrowed her eyes and glared at Sabina, feeling the slow heat begin to rise up from the pit of her stomach. "Looks as if you're not too picky about the company you're keeping these days." The words were out of Anna's mouth before she could stop them. The grin disappeared from Stefan's face. He looked as if he had shrunk several inches. Renata's face went from pale to ghostly. She shot Anna a terrified glance.

Sabina just snickered and then turned to walk away. The boys followed like obedient puppies.

"She can't be right about that, can she?" Stefan asked when Sabina was out of earshot. "How can they stop us from going to school?"

"I told you what my parents said," Renata whispered hoarsely, turning to face Anna. "Things are only going to get worse." Just then, the bell began to ring, summoning them to class. Renata turned to join the line entering the school building. Then she stopped. "He's a maniac, you know," she said over her shoulder. "Adolf Hitler."

The name of the German chancellor hung in the air like a bad smell. Anna realized with a start that that was exactly what her Baba had said.

The confrontation with Sabina, along with Renata's secret, stayed with Anna through the entire day. She wanted to talk to Renata after school. But her friend ran off, saying that her parents needed her to get home as quickly as possible. And Anna couldn't follow. She had to make her way to the music academy for her clarinet lesson. Her father had been teaching her to play since Anna was a child, almost too small to even hold the instrument that had been a gift from her mother. It was her prized possession. It was still just a bit too big for her small hands. Papa said the more she practiced, the more her fingers would grow and stretch. Usually, Anna had her music lessons at home. But sometimes, she would meet her father at the academy to take her lesson there and walk home with him.

Today especially, Anna longed to lose herself in the music lesson. Music would distract her from worrying about other things. And after the incident at Mr. Kaplansky's store, the disturbing conversation with Renata, and Sabina's ominous warning, it felt as if there was a lot to worry about!

She entered the academy and made her way down the long hallway. On her way to the rehearsal hall, she passed Mr. Zaleski, the janitor who worked in the building. He was a giant of a man, taller than anyone she knew, and with shoulders that were broad and hard from years of labor.

"Good afternoon, Miss Hirsch." Mr. Zaleski tipped his hat as he walked past. "Here for your lesson?" He had been seeing Anna come and go from this building for years.

"Yes," she replied. "But I'm just going to try to catch the last few minutes of my father's rehearsal." She hoped that Papa would still be inside the rehearsal hall, practicing with the orchestra. She often tried to arrive early on these lesson days so she could hear her father and the others play. She opened the door to the hall and slipped inside, closing it softly behind her. She was lucky. The orchestra members were in their seats and the rehearsal was still underway. Anna scanned the rows, searching for her father in the section with the other clarinets. Then she frowned. Papa was not in his usual seat. Where had he gone?

She was just about to leave the hall and go to her father's office when something caught her eye. At the back of the orchestra and off to one side, she noticed a small group of musicians. They had never been there before—completely separated from the rest of the players like that. And in the middle of that group sat Anna's father. *That's so strange,* she thought. Why was her papa seated at the back, and why were he and several other musicians so cut off from the others? Anna glanced at the people on her father's right and left. And then the truth began to dawn on her. And as she put these pieces together, the now familiar anxiety began to gnaw at her stomach once more. The small group of men and women next to her father were the Jewish musicians. They had all been segregated from the rest of the orchestra, set apart as if they had a contagious disease.

Anna had seen enough. She pushed her way out of the rehearsal hall and stumbled down the hallway. Her mind was reeling from the sight of her father in that penned-off section of the rehearsal hall. She felt truly frightened. She wanted to leave the building and run for the safety of home, even though she knew that she couldn't leave her father. Finally, she made her way to her father's office and sank into a chair. Papa found her there a few minutes later.

"Annichka!" he exclaimed when he walked in. "Yes, of course, your lesson is today." He seemed distracted and sounded as if he had forgotten. Anna looked up, seeing for the first time the worry that was creased around Papa's eyes. "I … um … the rehearsal went a bit longer than I thought. Have you been here for long? Here in the office, I mean." Even his voice sounded strained.

Anna opened her mouth to say something. She was desperate to know why the Jewish musicians were sitting apart from everyone else. But the look on her father's face stopped her. He was such a proud man, always so sure of himself. But suddenly he was fumbling for words and he couldn't seem to look her in the eye. Surely she couldn't ask about this new turn of events now, as it would embarrass him.

"No," she replied softly. "I just got here a few minutes ago. I thought I'd wait for you here."

Papa looked relieved. Anna had read him right. "Good," he replied with a deep sigh. "Let's start your lesson, then."

Anna reached for her clarinet, which she had brought with her. She placed her mouth on the mouthpiece and felt the reed against her bottom lip.

The reed was made of wood and was shaved down so finely at one end that it was as thin as tissue paper. When you held it up to the light, you could almost see through it. If there was the slightest crack or split in the reed, it was useless and, as her father always said, "they don't grow on trees, Anna." That always made her laugh because of course the reed did come from a tree! But she knew what Papa meant. The reed was special and needed to be treated carefully. But it also cost money. And even though Anna's family lived comfortably, they were careful with what they had to spend.

Anna applied light pressure to form a seal around the mouthpiece, just as her father always instructed her to, being careful to press only with her lips and not her teeth. She couldn't blow too hard or no air would pass through the wooden tube. Not too soft, either, or a perfect seal would not be formed. And then the only thing you'd hear would be air. She reached her hands around the tube, left hand on the keys on top and right hand on the bottom. The keys opened and closed as she applied pressure with her fingers. That's what changed the notes and created the tunes.

The reed vibrated slightly against her lower lip as she began to play for her father. She wanted to play like the soft wind that blew through Krakow in the spring. That would help lighten her spirit. And it would make her father happy. And maybe, if he loved the way she sounded, he would smile and she would take the sadness away from his eyes. But today, try as she might, the sounds that came from her clarinet were not the beautiful sounds she had hoped to make. Her mind was still elsewhere and not on the lesson. And Papa's face did not brighten.

"Again, Anna," Papa said. "Do the scale one more time."

A loud squawk came from her clarinet as Anna blew once more and moved her fingers over the keys. Today she knew that she sounded like a crow, screeching out a sound that made her father wince. *I'm Anna the crow—one of the barnyard animals*, she thought, lowering the clarinet to her side and staring at her father.

Normally, he would have said something about the way she was playing. He would have said, "I know what you are capable of doing, Annichka. I know you can play better than this." And Anna would have tried harder. But today, Papa looked as if he was barely listening to her. He had a faraway look on his face, and all he said was, "Again, please."

Anna raised the clarinet to her lips and began to play once more. She knew that she was still sounding like a crow squawking from a high wire. But Papa still did not comment. And that made her even more uneasy.

CHAPTER 6

The newspaper reported another attack on a Jewish store in the center of town. Papa tried to hide the paper from Anna when she came to the breakfast table, but she managed to get hold of it after he left for the music academy. The front-page headline in the paper was also unnerving. In bold black letters, it said, "Jobs and Bread for Poles, not Jews." *Aren't we Poles as well?* Anna wondered. She was perplexed to think how things were changing in her country in such a short amount of time—and all for the worse.

As always, she felt the need to talk to Renata. Who else but her best friend would be able to help her understand all of this? But when she arrived at the corner, Renata wasn't there to meet her. It had been a few mornings since Renata had been waiting for her.

Renata was still hiding something. It had been two weeks since she'd mentioned her secret, and while Anna didn't dare to press her about it, she could see Renata had grown quieter, walking around as if she were in a trance.

At school, Anna looked around for her, but it was Stefan who came walking up to her, grinning and pulling a face that reminded Anna of a circus clown. "You seem to be in a good mood," Anna said.

"And why not? I got the highest mark on yesterday's math test that I have ever received. Maybe I should become a mathematician—instead of a musician." Stefan grinned again.

Anna smiled. "The only reason you are doing so well in math is because Renata has been here to help. Without her, you'd be at the bottom of the heap!" She glanced around. Where *was* Renata, anyway? Today, there was no sign of Anna's friend. But thankfully no sign of Sabina either, or her bodyguards. After her outburst a couple of weeks earlier, Anna did not want to run into the police chief's daughter.

Stefan noticed Anna's eyes darting about the schoolyard. "My father said it's not possible to kick us out of school," he said. "Poland is not Germany. Adolf Hitler is not here. As much as I would love a break from school, I don't think it's going to happen."

"Don't be so sure, Stefan," Anna replied with some hesitation. "There are other things going on here that aren't good for us, either."

"Isolated incidents. That's what my father says as well. Just don't do anything to annoy Sabina. It's her goons I'm worried about—more than Hitler!"

"Don't worry," Anna replied. "I'm not looking for any trouble!"

Stefan sounded so sure of himself, and a part of Anna really wanted to believe him. It was true that Germany was not Poland. Perhaps nothing worse would happen here. But even as she wished this to be true, her mind was telling her something different.

"There's Renata." Stefan broke into Anna's thoughts. But why was she standing off by herself, across the schoolyard? Didn't she see them? "Renata!" Stefan shouted. When Renata still did not move, Anna and Stefan walked across the field to join her. "Didn't you hear me?" Stefan asked when they got close.

Renata looked up, her eyes puffy and red. She had been crying. Was that why she hadn't waited for Anna that morning? Was she avoiding her? This time, even Stefan could see that something was terribly wrong.

"What's happened?" he exclaimed. "You don't look very good."

Renata shook her head and didn't say a word.

"Are you sick?" he persisted. "Did Sabina say something to you again?"

"No," replied Renata hesitantly. "I'm not sick."

"Renata, you have to talk to us." Anna knew that she had promised Renata not to betray her secret—whatever it was. But enough was enough. "You can't keep acting as if something terrible has happened, and then say nothing."

Another moment passed before Renata finally spoke, and when she did, her voice was so soft Anna had to lean forward to hear her. "We're leaving."

Anna shook her head. "You're what?"

"We're going away."

"Going where? Are you going on a holiday?" Even as Stefan asked the question, Anna knew that wasn't possible. There were no school vacations coming up. And no one missed school unless they were sick.

"We're leaving for Denmark. We're getting out of here while we still can."

And with that, the gears finally clicked into place for Anna. Renata and her family were escaping, fleeing from signs that told Jews to stay away and from thugs on the street who might hurt them, and from whatever else was going to happen in Poland. That was the secret that Renata had been keeping to herself.

"I've been telling you that my parents are afraid things are going to get worse," Renata said. "They want to get out before that happens."

Anna stood mutely. Even Stefan said nothing.

"It's so complicated," Renata said, squeezing her eyes shut. "And it's not easy to leave. It's almost impossible these days for Jews to go anywhere in the world." She explained that without special papers, no one could leave their home country. "And there aren't many countries in the world that want to let Jews in. Did you even know that?" She stared deeply into Anna's eyes. Anna shook her head. Were they becoming stuck here in Poland?

"My father thinks we should just stay put," Stefan jumped in. "He says the trouble will pass."

Stefan was repeating himself. But this time, Anna didn't think he sounded convincing when he said the last part. And she wasn't convinced, either.

"I'm not sure how my parents got all the travel documents. They've been keeping all of that from me, and they made me swear not to say a word to anyone." She turned once more to Anna. "That's why I couldn't say anything to you." She stared deeply into Anna's eyes as she said this.

"When are you leaving?" Anna croaked out this question.

"In a week."

So soon!

"We're only taking a few suitcases with us. I've barely had any time to go through my things."

Anna wondered how you could possibly pack your whole life up and leave on a week's notice. "I ... I don't know what to say, Renata. You're my best friend." Anna felt completely helpless in the face of Renata's announcement.

"I'll miss you so much, Anna," Renata whispered. "And you, Stefan."

"I hope everything goes well for you, Renata," Stefan replied.

Anna was still searching for something to say. A part of her wanted to beg Renata to stay. But another part wondered if Renata's family was doing what they all should be doing—leaving while they could. "This isn't good-bye, Renata," she finally blurted. "Not yet." Then, blinking back tears, she reached over and gave her friend a hug, not trusting herself to say another word.

CHAPTER 7

When Anna arrived home from school, Baba was putting groceries away in the kitchen. Anna slumped down at the kitchen table and laid her head in her arms. Baba was by her side in an instant.

"What's wrong, Annichka? Are you not feeling well?" Baba pressed her hand to Anna's forehead.

"I'm fine, Baba." Anna looked up at her grandmother. It was true that she never wanted to worry Baba. She was wonderful, but mostly she just hovered in the background, ready to pop a bite of cake into Anna's mouth. Or ready to move in if Papa became too strict with Anna about her practicing. It was difficult to really talk to her. Still, Baba was like their guard dog, always on the lookout for trouble. She may have been the quiet one, but she would know if something was up. She might be the one to make sense of this.

"I heard some bad news today," Anna began.

Baba looked alarmed. "What news? Is someone *else* sick?"

"No, no one is sick. It's Renata. She told me that she's leaving Poland."

"Leaving?"

Anna nodded. "For good. Her parents want to get out before things get worse for Jews. They think that's going to happen."

Baba sucked in her breath and looked away.

"Baba, what do you think about the things that have been happening lately?"

"Hmm?" Baba left Anna's side and began moving around the kitchen, pulling out pots that she was going to use for that evening's supper. "What things?"

"You know what I'm talking about. You know what's going on in the world. You heard Hitler on the radio the other night. Those things." Baba may not have been one for long conversations, but Anna knew that she kept up with events in Poland and in neighboring Germany. Sometimes Anna caught her reading the newspaper late at night.

Baba glanced over at her. "There's no reason to worry," she said. "Everything will be fine." And then she brought the back of her right hand up to her mouth and pretended to spit onto her fingers three times, making a little popping sound: "Puh, puh, puh." Spitting three times was a Jewish superstition that was meant to prevent anything bad from happening. Baba did it all the time, whenever she mentioned anything good or bad. No matter what, you didn't want to encourage the evil spirits to appear.

"But what do you really think? Aren't you afraid?"

Baba hesitated before speaking. That alone made Anna nervous. She would have felt better if Baba had shouted "No!"

"I trust your father," Baba finally said. "He will not let anything happen to us."

Anna trusted him too. But she worried that even Papa, with all his wisdom, was not seeing everything that was happening under their noses—or at least not admitting it.

"Baba," she began, "I need to ask you about something, something that I saw a couple of weeks ago when I went to the academy to meet Papa."

Baba's eyes grew fearful, as if she knew what was coming. There was no stopping Anna now. She began to tell her grandmother about her father's extended rehearsal that she had stumbled into. She told Baba about Papa and the other Jewish musicians who had been relegated to a separate section of the orchestra. "Only the Jewish musicians, Baba—no one else was moved like that. Why would that happen?"

Baba looked away again.

"Did you even know about it?"

"Perhaps you should ask your father about this," Baba said, sighing deeply.

Anna would not be deterred. "No! I'm asking you. Tell me what's going on. Please!"

Baba sighed again. "Yes," she finally said. "Your father told me about this several weeks ago."

Several weeks! Maybe even before what happened at Mr. Kaplansky's.

"They are calling them ghetto chairs," Baba continued.

Anna knew a little bit—not a lot—about ghettos. Papa had once told her about a place in Italy where Jews were kept in separate areas, apart from others, as if they weren't good enough to be together. The ghetto in Italy had been established hundreds of years earlier, but it sounded just like what had happened to Papa and the other Jewish musicians.

"It's terrible that they should treat your father, such a respected musician, in this way! It's an insult to him—to all of us." Baba moaned and looked up to the skies as if she were begging for someone to help.

"Why didn't someone tell me?"

"A young person shouldn't have to worry about these things," Baba replied.

"But I'm not a baby. And do you think if you don't say anything, then I won't see what's happening? I see it, Baba. I listen to the radio. I read the newspaper. I hear things at school." Anna didn't want to tell her grandmother about Sabina's warning. She had said enough and heard enough, for now. "Sorry, Baba," she added, noting the distress on Baba's face. "I don't mean to shout. But I need to understand what's going on."

At that, Baba walked over to Anna and sat heavily into a chair next to her. She reached over to pull her granddaughter in for a long hug. "You are so much like your mother," she said, whispering into Anna's ear. "You are smart, as she was, and you have a big heart. She would be so proud of you." Anna loved hearing this. She loved it when anyone compared her to her mother, whom she missed more than she could say. Like her mother, Anna had thick curly hair that was framed against porcelain skin and eyes as big and round as full moons. Sometimes Papa told her that she was looking more and more like her mother with each passing day.

Baba released Anna and stood up, returning to

her pots and food preparation. "As long as we stay together as a family, then nothing bad will happen to us," she said. Then she spit three more times onto her fingers. Anna stood up from the kitchen table and headed for her bedroom. She wasn't sure if Baba could really keep the evil spirits away. They felt closer than ever.

CHAPTER 8

In her room, Anna flopped down on her bed and gazed at the wall where a number of pressed and framed flowers were hanging. After her clarinet, these pressed flowers were Anna's most important treasure. She had been collecting flowers for years, pressing them between her father's big music textbooks and mounting them on heavy paper. Papa had framed the ones on her wall. He called them little works of art. Anna wasn't sure about that, but she did think they were beautiful. Each flower had come from a special place: a pink carnation that her father had given her when she turned twelve, a lily from Renata's garden when they used to play there after school, and a rose she had taken, with Baba's permission, from the pots of flowers that she grew in front of the house. But her favorite flowers in the collection were two red poppies. Their color was so vibrant that they practically glowed on her wall. She had found these during a family holiday to the mountains when her mother was still alive. Usually, when Anna focused on her flower collection, she could lose herself in the memory of those happy times. But this afternoon, the sight of her flowers did nothing to ease her troubled mind.

Mr. Kaplansky's store, Papa and his ghetto chairs, Sabina's threat. And now Renata! Could things get any worse? Or, like a passing storm, would all of this blow over and life return to normal? Stefan had said that his family believed that the trouble in Poland would pass. Renata's family thought things were so bad they should leave. Who was right? And what did all of this mean for Anna? And then another thought hit her. Even if they did leave, where would they go? Renata had said it was difficult to get the papers needed to get out of Poland. But she also said that few countries anywhere were willing to take in Jews. Oh, if only Anna had a crystal ball that could show her the future, show her what they should do.

That evening, the family sat together in the sitting room after dinner. Music from the phonograph played softly in the background. It was a lullaby by

Chopin, or maybe Mozart; Anna wasn't sure which. Papa was drinking some tea and reading the newspaper. Baba was stitching together some pieces of fabric for a tablecloth she was making. And Anna was doing her homework. The truth was she was not getting very far in the book she had been assigned to read. She had been staring at the very same page for nearly half an hour. She really didn't want to think about homework and school. Thinking about school reminded her too much of the fact that Renata was going to be leaving in a few days. Anna hadn't told her father about Renata yet. It was something she could barely face herself.

"Here's something that you might be interested in," Papa said, breaking into Anna's thoughts. He lowered his glass of tea and leaned forward. "Do you remember that concert we were starting to listen to on the radio a few weeks ago? We never got to hear the whole thing."

Remember? How could I forget? That was the night the horrible news announcement had come on the air, the one with Adolf Hitler screaming those hateful messages to the world.

"I started to tell you that the violinist was a famous musician named Bronislaw Huberman. Well, you'll never guess, but I just read that he is coming to Poland."

"What a coincidence," said Baba. "Is he coming to Krakow? I would love to hear him play."

"So would I," Papa replied. "But he's not here to give a concert. He's actually coming to recruit musicians for a new orchestra that he is putting together."

"A new orchestra in Poland?" Practically every major city in their country had an orchestra. Anna couldn't understand why they would need another one.

"Actually, this orchestra is being formed in the British Mandate of Palestine."

Anna knew little about Palestine except that it was very far away.

"Mr. Huberman is holding auditions for the orchestra."

The news of a new orchestra and these auditions didn't interest Anna very much until Papa said, "He's inviting Jewish musicians to try out."

At that, Anna sat up in her chair. "I don't understand. Why only Jewish musicians, Papa?"

Her father knit his brow together. "I'm not sure. I imagine that these musicians will accompany Mr. Huberman to Palestine."

At first, Anna wasn't sure she had heard right. Had Papa actually said that Jewish musicians were being given the chance to leave Poland for this faraway place called Palestine? All they had to do was

audition for this Mr. Huberman and get into his orchestra? Anna sat farther up in her chair, her mind
going a mile a minute. An idea was taking shape, the
pieces coming together like a jigsaw puzzle. Perhaps
this was the sign she had been searching for. And it
had been handed to her like a gift on her birthday.
She didn't have a crystal ball to look into the future.
But maybe, just maybe, this new orchestra in this faraway Palestine was an opportunity that her family
could not pass up, a signal that they should also pack
up and get out, just like Renata.

Papa needed to audition for this orchestra. And if
he got in, and Anna was certain he would, then her
family would have a chance to leave. And it would all
be thanks to this musician named Mr. Huberman.

"You're going to audition, aren't you, Papa?" Anna
blurted this question out.

Papa had returned to reading his newspaper.
Now, he lowered the paper and stared at Anna. He
looked confused. "What are you talking about?"
he asked.

"The orchestra that Bronislaw Huberman is putting together in Palestine. Don't you see? If you get
into this orchestra—I mean *when* you get in—then
we'll be able to leave here, and we'll have a place
to go."

"Annichka, where is this coming from? I have no intention of leaving Krakow."

"Papa, please just listen to me. And don't say anything until I'm finished talking. You too, Baba," she added when her grandmother made a move to leave the sitting room. Baba sank back in her chair. Her face grew pale. And with that, Anna spoke. The words poured out of her in a rush, like a balloon releasing all of its air. She reminded her father and Baba about everything she had read in the newspapers and heard on the radio about Jewish people who had been targeted in Poland. She reminded him about Mr. Kaplansky's store, this time emphasizing the part about police chief Zabek. She told them both about Sabina's warning that she and her Jewish friends would have to leave school. Finally, she told her father that Renata and her family were going.

By the time she was finished talking, Papa had removed his glasses and closed his eyes, pinching the bridge of his nose with his fingers as if he were in pain. Baba's eyes were wide open, darting furiously from Anna to her father and back again. The silence continued for several seconds while Anna tried to control her breathing and the pounding of her heart. She had said everything she wanted to say.

Finally, Papa straightened up and opened his eyes. He gazed at his daughter. He looked tired. "Annichka," he began, "l will not lie to you. I have been worried about some of the things you mentioned."

There! He finally said it! This admission was enormous.

"But ..."

Oh no, Anna thought, her heart sinking into her stomach.

"But," he said again, "what you are suggesting is simply impossible. We cannot abandon our lives and leave."

"Why not?" Anna jumped in. "Renata's family is going. I know it won't be easy," she added.

"Impossible!" Papa repeated, more forcefully. "Our home is here. My work is here. Your mother is even buried here." At that last part, his voice caught in his throat. Baba sniffled and blew loudly into a handkerchief. Papa continued. "I will not uproot our lives for something that is completely uncertain. I understand that things are perhaps feeling desperate for you, but I need you to try and keep a level head about all of this."

What does that even mean? Anna wondered. As far as she was concerned, she was being completely sensible. If things were dangerous, and Papa knew it, then leaving was the only option.

"I'm going to say this to you again, Annichka," Papa said, leaning forward. "So please listen to me. We are not in any danger."

"Then why is Renata leaving?" Anna asked.

Papa took a deep breath and stared at his daughter. "Some people have become overly fearful and feel they need to get away. But I'm not afraid." He said this last part even before Anna had a chance to ask him anything. "And you should not be afraid either. Besides," he added, "even if something worse were to happen to the Jews of Krakow, I am protected. I'm a member of the orchestra. Poland loves its musicians. So we are safe staying right here."

Anna stared evenly at her father. "I know about the ghetto chairs," she said. "Baba told me. And I saw you the last time I came to the academy for my lesson."

Papa glanced over at Anna's grandmother, who quickly averted her eyes. "I can live with being in a different seat in the orchestra," he said. "And no one has hurt us." Papa avoided Anna's stare when he said this last part.

"Not yet!" Anna blurted out.

Papa straightened up in his seat and put his glasses back on. "Nothing worse will happen here," he said.

"But how do you—"

Papa raised his hand and Anna stopped.

"Nothing worse," he repeated.

Anna looked away, not wanting to meet her father's eyes.

"Please, Annichka," he insisted. "You must trust me when I say this."

Anna turned to her grandmother. "If you had the chance to leave Poland today, Baba, would you do it?"

Baba, who had been rocking nervously in her seat, raised her head. "Why are you asking me these questions, Annichka?"

"Please answer me, Baba."

Baba hesitated and then said, "I can't imagine my life anywhere but here."

Anna persisted. "But given everything we know and everything I've said, would you go now if you had the chance?"

In Baba's eyes, Anna could see a flicker of something different—a seed of agreement even as she stammered out a response. "I-I think—I mean, I don't think …" And then her voice trailed off.

Just then, Papa jumped in again. "Annichka," he said, sounding even more tired than before. "We've all said enough. I think it's time for you to go to bed."

Anna felt the weight of failure on her shoulders. But as she rose from the table and left the sitting room, she realized that Baba had never answered her question about leaving. And in not answering, Baba had made her response to Anna loud and clear.

X

Before reaching her bedroom, Anna paused in the hallway to listen in on what was happening back in the sitting room. Baba, who had been silent during Anna's exchange with Papa, suddenly began to talk.

"I also think you should go to this audition," Baba was saying.

"There's no point," Anna heard her father reply.

"He's providing travel papers for the people he chooses for this orchestra, isn't he?" Baba asked. "That's why Jewish musicians are being invited to try out."

Anna strained to hear what her father would say, but he did not reply. Finally, Baba continued. "Families like ours would be able to leave here with papers. That's more valuable than gold these days."

"I just don't know," Papa replied. And then he said something that Anna had never heard him say before. "It frightens me to think about leaving here. We have built our whole lives here in Poland. How can I start again somewhere else?"

"Well, it frightens me to stay!" her grandmother exclaimed. Then there was another long silence before

Baba spoke again. "When Anna asked me if I would leave Poland if I had the chance, I avoided the question. I can't even face her and tell her what I'm really thinking. Neither can you."

So there it was! Papa was afraid to leave. And Baba wanted to go.

"I'm not going to leave our city," Papa said, raising his voice and then quickly lowering it. "I'm not going to pull Anna away from here and take her halfway across the world to some place that is not our home."

Anna pressed herself closer to the wall, eager to hear how her grandmother would reply to this. When Baba finally spoke, her voice was thick with emotion. And the woman who was usually so quiet suddenly found her strong voice.

"What is a home?" Baba asked. "Isn't it just a place where you feel safe? Tell me, my dear son, when was the last time you really felt safe here in Krakow?"

Anna had heard enough. She quickly retreated to her bedroom and closed the door softly behind her.

CHAPTER 9

In the wake of Papa's firm pronouncement that they would not leave Poland, a dark cloud descended on Anna. She felt as if all hope had been sucked away from her. Baba tried her best to brighten Anna's mood in the only way she knew—she prepared Anna's favorite desserts: thin and light-as-air crepes stuffed with jam, and moist apple cake. But not even those sweet treats could lift Anna's spirits.

What saddened her even more was that, as Renata's departure loomed nearer, Anna had been avoiding her friend: departing early for school so they wouldn't meet at the corner, dodging her in the playground or pulling Stefan into every conversation, and rushing out after school was done. Anna knew it wasn't fair for her to do that. But she just couldn't face Renata. She didn't know how to say good-bye. Well, there was no avoiding it any longer. Renata was leaving in a few days.

On Saturday morning, Anna made her way over to Renata's house. The wind that day was biting, but the sun shone so brightly that Anna had to shield her eyes from its glare. She trudged up the path to Renata's house and knocked on the door. Renata's mother answered a moment later.

"Anna, come in. Get out of that wind," Renata's mother exclaimed, pulling Anna by the arm into the front hallway of the house. "Please excuse this terrible mess. As Renata told you, we're leaving in two days and we're still sorting through everything to figure out what to take with us."

Anna glanced around the living room. It looked as if a cyclone had hit. Clothes were thrown over the couch and chairs, books were spread out across the floor and tables, and boxes were piled on top of one another.

"I know what you're thinking," Renata's mother continued before Anna had a chance to say anything. "Chaos, right? But I know where everything is, and we just need to organize it and start to pack. But what am I babbling about? You're here to see Renata." Then she lowered her voice and leaned in closer to Anna's face. "The thing that saddens me the most is separating the two of you. I wish there was something we could do about that. And I wish most of all that you were leaving too. But ..."

Anna gulped. She wished that as well.

"But," Renata's mother continued, "that's not my decision to make." Then she straightened. "Go to Renata. I know she's eager to see you."

Renata's room was as cluttered as the rest of the house. Renata stood in the middle of her floor, trying to sort through a mountain of dresses that was so high it threatened to topple over. Anna picked her way over sweaters and blouses. She was about to push a box aside when she heard a muffled noise coming from inside. She knelt down and opened the box, and there was Renata's dog staring up at her and whimpering softly.

"Bestia," Anna cried. "Have you found a new spot to hide?" She reached down and scratched under the dog's chin and it perked up its ears. The dog had come into Renata's life when it was a puppy and she was an infant. They had grown up together. But it was the name that always made Anna smile. *Bestia* meant *the beast*. This dog was anything but ferocious. It was about as cowardly as any animal could be. It didn't surprise Anna to see Bestia hiding in this dark place.

"He knows something is going on," Renata said, coming to stand next to Anna. "And he knows he's not part of it."

"What's going to happen to him?"

"Our neighbor is taking him. I know she loves him almost as much as I do. And I know he'll be fine. But it's something else that I can't bear to think about." Then she turned to face Anna. "You've been avoiding me."

Anna nodded. "I'm sorry. I didn't know what to say. I'm just so sad that you're going."

"Me too."

"I have something for you," Anna said. She had thought long and hard about what she wanted to give Renata when she left. And that morning, she had come up with the perfect gift. She reached into her pocket, pulled out one of the dried red poppies that was part of her pressed flower collection, and held it out to Renata.

"But it's your favorite!"

"And that's why I want you to have it," Anna replied. "Not that you'll need anything to remember me, because we'll always be friends no matter where we are. But I want you to hang this on your wall in your new home and think of me."

Renata held the framed flower in her hands as if it were a fragile piece of china. "Do you remember when you tried to get me interested in making these? What a mess I made."

"Art was never your thing," Anna said.

"And math was never yours."

"But together, we're a perfect team." They chanted that last line in unison, like a hymn.

"What am I going to do without you?" Anna began to cry.

"I'll write. I promise. And you have to swear you'll do the same."

It would have to do, Anna thought, gulping back tears and nodding. "And who knows?" Renata continued. "Maybe we'll end up in the same place at some point."

It was then that Anna told her friend about the orchestra being formed in Palestine by the famous violinist.

"You have to convince your father to go," Renata said. "I would feel so much better about leaving if I knew you were also going somewhere safer."

"I don't know what it's going to take. Right now, he's determined to stay."

The silence that filled the room was heavy. Anna knew that there was nothing Renata could say that would help her. Convincing her father to leave seemed to be resting on her shoulders alone.

"I have something for you, as well," Renata said. She spun around and began to rummage through another pile of clothing. When she turned back to Anna, she was holding a scarf in her hands—the green silk one she had been wearing the day the girls had witnessed Mr. Kaplansky's store being vandalized. "I told you it would look good with anything you wear. I want you to have it."

Anna took the scarf from Renata's hands and wrapped it slowly around her neck. "How does it look?"

"Perfect." And then Renata's voice broke and she turned away again. "My mother is limiting the number of dresses I can take," she said. Anna could see her furiously brushing away the tears that were streaming down her cheeks. "But how will I ever choose?"

"I'll help you," Anna replied. "We're still a team. Don't forget that."

CHAPTER 10

How was it possible to go from seeing her best friend every day to not seeing her at all, and maybe never seeing her again? Renata's empty desk was a constant reminder of her absence. Anna became even quieter over the next days and weeks, and not even Stefan with his jokes and smiles could pull Anna's low spirits up. It didn't help that Sabina had started to taunt her again whenever they saw each other on the playground. Even without her goons to protect her, Sabina would hurl threats at Anna.

"Your days at school are numbered," she said one day.

"That friend of yours may have gotten out, but you won't be so lucky," she said another time. One day, she even said that it wouldn't be long before Papa lost all his students. Anna tried to stay as far away from her as possible, but it wasn't always easy.

Several days later, as Anna was walking home from school, she could hear the sounds of a brawl nearby, even before she could see what was happening. Angry voices rose and dropped in a unified swell. Here and there, a solitary outburst cut through the crowd. "Get him!" someone shouted. "Don't stop," another echoed. And then the others joined in to cheer once more.

She knew she shouldn't get any closer. She was already late getting home and Baba would start to worry. But something inside of her was propelling her forward instead of toward the safety of her home, even as Baba's troubled face appeared in her mind. *I'll stop for a second, just to see what's happening,* she thought, curiosity overtaking her. The sounds close to the crowd were so much louder. Anna raised herself up on her tiptoes, straining to see above the heads of those who were pressed together in front of her, closer than the bricks in the wall of her home. From the back of the horde, she couldn't see a thing. So she plunged into the crowd, elbowing past women with their arms raised in the sky and men who thumped their fists into their open palms. The sight that greeted her at the front made her blood run cold.

The same boys who had painted the Star of David on Mr. Kaplansky's store were there again. But his time, they did not have paint tins in their hands. This was so much worse. This time, they were there to hurt the butcher. The thugs had pushed Mr. Kaplansky to the ground. They were taunting and mocking him, shoving his feet out from under him every time he tried to stand. He fumbled with shaking hands to keep his glasses on his face. But his skullcap had fallen off his head and he was desperately trying to retrieve it. The young hoodlums would have none of that. "What's the matter, old man? Can't pray without this thing on your head?" The oldest-looking boy in the mob picked up the skullcap and dangled it in front of Mr. Kaplansky's face.

Sabina Zabek's father stood close by, just as he had the previous time. His hands were on his hips, his belly bursting out of his uniform. And just like before, he was watching and doing nothing. Anna turned her head this way and that, praying that someone, anyone, would step in to help Mr. Kaplansky. No one came forward.

The crowd continued to shout, "Get him! Get him! Get him!" while Anna's heart thumped along with the beat of their jeers. She was frozen on the spot. Her face was hot, and a slow tremor was rising up through her legs and spreading across the rest of her body. She raised a shaking hand and was just about to reach it out to Mr. Kaplansky when she felt someone snap her arm back to her side. Anna looked up into a familiar face. It was Mr. Zaleski, the janitor at the music academy. What was Mr. Zaleski doing here? Was he here to help or also to cause trouble? He knew that Anna was Jewish. Would he reveal that to the thugs? Anna knew that this crowd would not hesitate to turn on her as well, even though she was only a young girl. *Why did I stop here?* Anna moaned silently as Mr. Zaleski leaned down until his face was only inches away from hers.

"Go home, Miss Hirsch!" Mr. Zaleski warned in a low but urgent tone. "Quickly, before anyone else sees you. You don't want to be here."

Mr. Kaplansky was moaning on the ground. Anna yearned to help him, but she knew there was nothing she could do. The crowd was getting uglier and more riled up by the second.

"Go!" Mr. Zaleski's voice cut through Anna's thoughts.

With one more helpless look at Mr. Kaplansky, Anna turned and pushed through the crowd. She ran, without looking back, until she reached her home.

CHAPTER 11

Anna flew through the doors of her house and straight into Baba's arms. Her hands were shaking uncontrollably and her breathing came in shallow gulps. It was several seconds before she could control her body. In the meantime, Baba looked as if she might pass out.

"Annichka!" Baba shrieked. "What's wrong? Are you hurt? Are you sick? Please, you must talk to me. You're scaring me!"

It was several more seconds before Anna could say anything, and when she finally began to speak, the words came pouring out of her in a continuous stream. It didn't matter anymore that this was Baba and Anna had always felt the need to protect her. The scene she had witnessed on the street was so completely overwhelming, so terrifying, that nothing could stop her from pouring out her heart. Baba's face fell and then fell some more as Anna described seeing the boys from her school push and hurt Mr. Kaplansky.

"And this was the second time, Baba!" Anna cried. "I don't understand why they were going after him like that."

Baba opened her mouth as if she was going to respond, but Anna wasn't finished yet.

"And the police chief! He seemed to be enjoying the whole thing. Everyone on the street was acting as if this was okay—as if they wanted more. Mr. Kaplansky didn't do anything wrong. *We* haven't done anything wrong. So why is this happening?" On and on Anna went, until finally, she ran out of words and ran out of energy. Then she simply slumped exhausted against Baba and held on with all her might.

Baba squeezed back, rocking Anna in her arms just as she used to do when Anna was a child and had hurt herself on the playground. In those days, a simple hug would have quickly taken away the pain, made everything fine again. If only that were the case today.

"Thank goodness you're safe, Annichka," Baba finally said after she had rocked and held Anna for the longest time. "And we must talk to your father about all of this. He must know what happened."

Anna pulled away from her grandmother. "I know what Papa's going to say. He's going to tell me to keep my head down and stay away from any trouble. He's going to say that nothing is going to happen to us. But he doesn't know that. He *can't* know that! Look what happened to Mr. Kaplansky!"

The truth was that Anna couldn't talk to her father these days, not since their argument about leaving Poland. The man who had always been so strong and outspoken had become quiet, shrinking away from his daughter just like he had in the months following her mother's death.

"Your papa is very troubled by everything, Annichka. He may not talk about it but I know he's worried."

Being worried just wasn't enough as far as Anna was concerned. And maybe the time for talking had passed. It was time to take action. And there was only one solution that Anna could see.

"Baba, do you remember that violinist, Mr. Huberman, the one who is coming to Poland? I just know that it would solve everything if Papa would agree to audition for him. But so far, Papa has refused to even think about leaving here."

"I've thought so much about that orchestra as well," Baba replied.

"You have?"

Baba nodded, and then looked away as if she was deep in thought. Finally, she turned back. "You know," she began, "maybe there is a way to get your father to go."

"But how? He won't consider going to an audition. He won't even write a letter to Mr. Huberman to ask for one."

"Perhaps he doesn't have to."

What was Baba talking about? Of course Papa had to write a letter. As good a musician as he was, no one was going to spontaneously request that he appear in front of Mr. Huberman. Everyone had to apply. It was as simple as that.

Baba smiled. "What I mean is perhaps we can ask *for* him."

"You mean that we should write to Mr. Huberman for Papa?"

"That's exactly what I mean."

Anna paused and then smiled along with her grandmother. It was the perfect solution. Why hadn't she thought of it? She stood up, and without saying a word, she ran to her bedroom to get some writing paper. When she returned, Baba was already seated at the desk, pen in hand.

"I saved the newspaper from the night your father told us about Mr. Huberman," Baba said. "The information about the audition is there. I thought perhaps it might come in handy."

Baba was surprising Anna more and more by the minute. But when it came time to compose the letter, Baba held the pen out to Anna. "You write it, Annichka," she pleaded. "I can't put these words together. And I don't know if this famous man will listen to an old woman like me."

Anna considered that for a moment. Would Mr. Huberman pay attention to the appeal of a young girl? She didn't think so. "You're wrong, Baba. You're the one to write it." Baba hesitated. "I'll help you," Anna added.

Baba finally nodded in agreement, and the two of them began to discuss what to include in the letter. Baba wanted to add all the details of what was happening to Jews in Krakow.

"I'm sure Mr. Huberman knows these things," Anna pointed out. "Why else would he be forming this orchestra to get Jewish musicians out of the country?"

Anna wanted to let Mr. Huberman know that many people were leaving Krakow just like Renata. But Baba thought that they should focus only on themselves and their wish to go. It had to be simple and to the point.

Dear Mr. Huberman,
I am the mother of Avrum Hirsch and I live in
Krakow with my son and granddaughter. My son
is a great clarinetist who teaches at the music
academy and plays in the Krakow Philharmonic
Orchestra. I know that you are holding auditions
for a new orchestra that will be formed in Palestine.
I would like you to consider allowing my son to be
part of that orchestra.

Baba paused and read back what she had written so far. That was the formal part of the letter. But now they needed to explain to Mr. Huberman the more personal part.

I don't think I have to tell you that it is becoming
harder for Jewish families like ours to feel safe in
Krakow. My granddaughter has seen things that no
child should be seeing. My son thinks that we will be
fine and the danger will pass. But I don't believe that
is true. Being a part of your new orchestra would give
my family a chance to start over in a safer place.

You may have guessed by now that my son doesn't
even know that I am writing this letter. But I know
that if he gets an audition, he will be there!

Anna read the whole thing out loud when Baba was finished writing. "I think there's one more thing you should add," she said. "'Please allow my son, Avrum Hirsch, to come and play for you. YOU WON'T REGRET IT!'"

She asked Baba to put the last sentence in capital letters so Mr. Huberman would know how serious they were. Then they read through what Baba had written one more time, and when they were satisfied that they had said everything they wanted to say, Baba signed the letter—*With gratitude, Mrs. Helena Hirsch*—folded it up, and placed it in an envelope, addressing it according to the instructions in the newspaper article.

"We don't have to tell your father anything about this. Not yet, anyway," Baba said as she licked a stamp and placed it in the corner of the envelope. "Not that I want to keep secrets from him," she added quickly.

"Agreed," Anna said. She and Baba decided they would not say a word to Papa about their letter unless they heard back from Mr. Huberman. Until, then, they would wait.

Chapter 12

Weeks passed, and one day Papa asked Anna to accompany him to the academy so that he could gather some music he needed for his students. She was reluctant to go. She still had a lingering image of the janitor, Mr. Zaleski, who had been there in the middle of the horde that was attacking Mr. Kaplansky weeks earlier. Even though Mr. Zaleski had warned her to get out of there, a kernel of doubt remained in her mind about his intentions. *Why had he been standing at the front of the mob to begin with? Is he one of them or one of us?* But Papa seemed so desperate for her company, and they had not spent much time together in weeks. In the end, she felt she couldn't turn him down. On the way to the academy, Anna found a couple of pale blue and purple crocuses. They were the only colorful flowers in an otherwise ugly, brown patch of dirt—a little burst of life growing by the side of the road. She had plucked them and already had plans to press them when she got home.

The hallways of the academy were deserted on this Sunday morning. As Anna waited outside her father's office for him to collect his sheet music, she spied Mr. Zaleski at the far end of the building. He was meticulously cleaning the halls, as he did every weekend. The wood floors shone like an ice skating rink, and were just as slippery. Mr. Zaleski's mop made a squeaking sound as he glided it across the floors. He looked up and called out to her.

"Good morning, Miss Hirsch." He lowered his mop to one side as he approached and pushed the cap he was wearing back on his head as he scratched at his forehead. "I was hoping that someone would arrive to help me clean this place. Are you my helper?"

He was trying to be playful, greeting her as if nothing had happened between the two of them. "Good morning, Mr. Zaleski," Anna replied, respectfully but warily.

The janitor came close to where Anna was standing. She glanced over her shoulder into Papa's office. What was taking him so long?

"Miss Hirsch?" Mr. Zaleski leaned toward Anna. "I want you to know something … about that day."

Anna's back stiffened. How was he going to explain himself? Why was he lowering his voice?

Mr. Zaleski looked around as if someone might be listening, and then he said, "You have to know that I waited on the street that day until everyone had left, and then I helped Mr. Kaplansky to his feet and walked him home." Mr. Zaleski's voice became even softer. "I was there to help, Miss Hirsch. But I knew I couldn't take the mob on by myself."

At first, Anna didn't respond. She stared at Mr. Zaleski as the realization of what he had just said hit her. He was on their side. He was a friend, just as she had hoped.

"Thank you," she finally blurted out as she exhaled a long, deep breath. "That means a lot."

The janitor grinned—a smile that stretched across his face. "So," he continued, "will you help me with the floors, or not?"

This time, Anna laughed. "No, not today, Mr. Zaleski. But I don't think you need my help. I can practically see my reflection in the floor. And it's blinding me." She squinted at the floor and then shielded her eyes for effect.

Mr. Zaleski chuckled. "My wife says I can clean a

floor better than she can. Well, if you're not here to help me, then may I ask what you are doing here? Just because I'm stuck indoors, I don't think you need to be. A young girl like you needs to be out with friends."

At that moment, Anna's father emerged from his office, papers in hand.

"Oh, Mr. Hirsch." Mr. Zaleski straightened, removed his cap, and bowed respectfully to Anna's father.

"Good morning, Mr. Zaleski. Are you well? How are your wife and children?"

"All very well, sir," Mr. Zaleski replied. "Is there anything I can get for you?" He placed his mop in a broom closet that was next to Papa's office.

Papa placed his papers into his briefcase. "I think I have everything that I need right here. Anna came along for company today. But I think we will head home now. Don't work too hard, Mr. Zaleski."

Just then, they heard a bang. The front door at the end of the hallway had opened and shut, and inside the building now stood four young men who began to walk the length of the passage toward them. Even at a distance, Anna could see the angry sneers on their faces. They staggered slightly, falling together and then shoving one another to stand up straight as they strode down the hall. Anna had seen men stagger like that when they came out of the pubs in town. She knew immediately that they did not belong in the academy. And as she peered more closely, she realized that a couple of them were the same thugs from her school who had beaten up Mr. Kaplansky weeks earlier. She sucked in her breath. Her grip tightened on the flowers that she was still holding in one hand. Papa stiffened and instinctively stepped in front of her. As she peered around from behind his back, Mr. Zaleski turned and followed their gaze. He called out to the young men. "What do you want here? This building is closed for the weekend."

The four of them paused, swaying slightly as they stood in the middle of the corridor. One, the tallest of the group, replied, "We thought we might catch a few Jews in here. Isn't that one standing behind you?"

From the way they were slurring their words, Anna was certain they were drunk.

Mr. Zaleski placed his hands on his hips, filling the hallway with his bulk. "Get out of here," he said loudly and with authority. "This is no place for hooligans like you."

The thugs did not move. The tall one spoke once again. "Look," he said as he threw his arm around the shoulder of one of his partners. "The Jew is hiding behind an old janitor. He's a coward, just like all of them."

Anna felt her father step forward. No one would ever call him a coward. And at that very same moment, the thugs began to walk briskly toward them, fists clenched and raised in the air. Panic dug into Anna's heart. She imagined that in another minute, she and her father would find themselves on the floor and cowering under the thrashing that these young men were about to dole out. They wouldn't care that her father was a respected musician or that she was a child. Closer and closer they came, narrowing the space in between them. She could hear them grunting; she could see the scowls on their faces; she could almost smell their rage. Twenty steps more, then ten, then five. She braced herself and was just about to cover her face with her hands for protection when Mr. Zaleski turned toward her and Papa. He grabbed Anna with one arm and Papa with the other, practically lifting them off their feet. The flowers that Anna had been carrying fell to the floor. Without a word, Mr. Zaleski shoved Anna and her father into the broom closet. The door slammed behind them and they were immediately enveloped in darkness. Anna heard a key turn in the lock.

A second later, she heard pounding on the door. Someone jiggled the handle and called out, "Come out, Jews. Or are you too afraid?" The voice taunted them.

Anna pressed up as close to her father as she could get, afraid that the thugs would force the door open. Papa encircled her with one arm and squeezed her against his side until she almost cried out in pain. In the darkness, she couldn't see his face, but from the trembling of his hand, she knew that he had to be feeling scared too. And as terrified as she was for their safety, she was equally afraid for Mr. Zaleski. She couldn't hear his voice on the other side of the door. Had these horrible young men hurt him? She remembered what he had said about taking on a mob. Even with his strength and size, how could he possibly fend off four people?

And then she heard talking, snatches of conversation, and she leaned up close to the door to be able to hear what was being said on the other side. The first thing she heard was Mr. Zaleski's voice.

"Why hurt a child?" he was saying, obviously trying to calm the men down. "There are bigger fish in the sea."

There was a muted response that Anna couldn't make out, and then, what sounded like a scuffle. She heard a thud as if someone had fallen to the ground and more angry voices grunting and snorting. She wasn't sure, but she thought she heard someone say, "Take that!" And then another voice demanded,

"Where's the key?" The muffled grunts and thumps continued for several more minutes. And then there was silence. The fighting seemed to have stopped, and a moment later, footsteps receded down the hall. Still, Anna and her father remained in the broom closet, pressed against each other for what felt like forever. Neither one of them spoke. Anna leaned closer to the door, and finally, she heard another set of footsteps, softer this time. A key turned in the lock. She held her breath as the door squeaked open. Mr. Zaleski was standing on the other side.

His face was ghostly white, except for an angry red welt just under one eye. His hands that held the key were shaking so much the keys were jingling.

"They've gone," Mr. Zaleski said. His voice trembled almost as much as his hands.

Anna and her father tumbled out of the broom closet and Anna rushed toward the janitor. "Are you all right? Did they hurt you?" She was shaking from head to toe, and realizing how close she and Papa had come to being beaten ... or worse! And Mr. Zaleski had been the one to save her, again! It was taking all of her control to keep herself from breaking down in tears.

Mr. Zaleski reached up to touch his eye, gently probing around his cheek and forehead. "They just needed to hit someone—blow off some steam. I'm fine. No need to worry, Miss Hirsch," he added when he saw Anna's stricken face. "This time, I got in a few punches myself."

"Shall we call your wife?" Papa asked. "Shall we walk you home? Or to the doctor?"

Mr. Zaleski shook his head. "No, please, I'm quite fine." He touched the welt again. "This will be gone in a few days."

"Well at least come and sit down." Papa tried to take Mr. Zaleski by the arm and lead him into his office, but the janitor would have none of it. No matter what they said, Mr. Zaleski would not accept any help from them.

"How we can thank you for saving us?" Papa asked hoarsely.

Mr. Zaleski lowered his hand from his face and stared at Anna and her father. "Please, go home, Mr. Hirsch," he said. "And you too, young miss. The streets are not a good place for you. You can thank me by staying safe."

Anna glanced down at her feet. The beautiful crocuses she had picked earlier that day were lying on Mr. Zaleski's polished floor, crushed and broken in the skirmish that had taken place. Papa took Anna by the hand, and together, they walked out of the building. When they were on the street, Anna pulled her father's arm and he turned to look at her.

"It's time, Papa," she said. "You can't say no anymore. We've written to Mr. Huberman—Baba and me—and asked for an audition into his orchestra for you. We need to leave."

Papa stared long and hard at Anna. Finally, he nodded his head and the two of them marched in silence, placing one foot in front of the other until they arrived at home and walked in the door. Baba was waiting for them, and she eyed them up and down as if she knew something terrible had just happened.

"I told him," Anna blurted out. "I told Papa that we wrote to Mr. Huberman."

At that, Baba placed one arm around Anna's shoulders and the other on Papa's arm, pulling them close to her as if to say that they were all in this together. She had a determined look in her eyes that Anna had never seen before. Papa stared back, first at Anna, and then at Baba. Then he simply said, "I hope we hear from him soon."

When Mr. Huberman's invitation for Papa to audition finally arrived, Anna felt a surge of joy that she had not felt in some time. The audition was being held in the city of Warsaw, which was quite far from Krakow, many miles away. The train ride would take over three hours. Anna begged Papa to let her go with him, desperate to hear her father audition and hoping to catch a glimpse of this Mr. Huberman, who was going to get them out of Krakow to make a new home in this country called Palestine. Papa wasn't so sure about taking her, but Anna had persisted, and he finally gave in. They would have to leave at the crack of dawn.

As eager as she was to go, Anna was also nervous about taking the train. After the encounter with the

thugs at the music academy, she worried that someone on the train might also harass them. But in the
end, the train ride was uneventful, and after several
sleepy hours, they arrived in Warsaw and made their
way to the National Theater concert hall.

This was the second time that Anna had been to
this theater. Her father had brought her here once
before to listen to a concert he was playing in along
with the Krakow orchestra. Papa had gotten Anna
and Baba seats in the balcony. And even though it was
close to the back of the theater and far from the stage,
Anna hadn't minded. She went to all of Papa's concerts. He usually performed at the Juliusz Slowacki
Theatre—the grandest theater in all of Krakow. And
even if she sat in the very last row and couldn't see
over the tall hats of the women who dressed to the
nines, she still heard it all. That was the most important thing. The sounds were enough to create
all kinds of images in Anna's mind. Sometimes the
music swelled and it reminded her of a storm blowing
through the city. Other times the notes were as soft
and as light as butterflies floating on air. And occa-
sionally, the sound was as playful as a litter of
kittens. She could close her eyes and imagine all of
that and more. That was the best thing about going
to a concert. It was the listening.

Anna and her father entered the concert hall and were directed to a room behind the stage that had been reserved for the musicians, many of whom were already there tuning up. Anna guessed there had to be over a hundred performers holding oboes, trumpets, basses, cellos, and violins. She gulped as she looked around. Anna believed that her father was one of the finest performers in the country. But she hadn't realized how many others also wanted to use this opportunity to get out of Poland. There was so much riding on this chance. *What if this Mr. Huberman doesn't choose Papa? What will happen to us then?*

"Anna," Papa said, as he began to unpack his clarinet. "You will wait for me here while I go onstage to play for Mr. Huberman."

What? "But I thought I could come with you and listen. I'll be quiet as can be."

Papa shook his head. "I'm afraid that only the musicians are allowed in the concert hall."

The frustration exploded inside of Anna. What was she supposed to do while he went onstage? Pace this room from side to side and wonder what was happening? Their fate would be decided inside the theater, and she wouldn't even get to be there to witness it. *This is so unfair!*

At that moment, Anna noticed a boy about her

age who was sitting in a chair off to the side. He was the only other young person in the room, and she decided it was the perfect opportunity to try and make a friend. He might have some information about the audition process and what to expect. Papa looked so nervous that she didn't want to bother him by asking too much. Instead, she walked up to this boy and he rose from his seat. They gazed at each other, sizing each other up. He was taller than her by about a half a head. His arms and legs were long and awkward, as if they had grown too fast for his body. His hair was orange, the color of autumn leaves, and he had freckles across his nose to match. His glasses hid eyes that were a deep green.

"We play the trumpet," he said, breaking the silence. He pointed to his father, a rather stern-looking, tall man with a perfectly trimmed beard, and the only other person in the room with orange hair. He was blowing easy runs on his instrument. How odd that this boy had said "we" as if he were also auditioning. And he sounded so solemn, especially when she compared him to Stefan, who was always kidding around. She wondered if this boy was any good on the trumpet or whether he would sound like one of the animals in her father's barnyard student orchestra.

"Clarinet," Anna replied, pointing to her father. He was pacing in a circle, round and round. That only happened when he was about to face something really important. The sight of Papa looking so anxious brought a chill down Anna's spine.

"I'm Eric Sobol." The boy bowed slightly in her direction. Anna stifled a giggle. He was so proper and formal—and dressed in a suit and tie. Mind you, Baba had insisted that Anna also wear her best dress that was reserved for special occasions, with the shiny black shoes that always pinched her toes. "If Mr. Huberman sees you, he will know that we are a good family," Baba had said. At the last minute, Anna had added the green scarf that Renata had given her—a good-luck charm, she hoped!

Anna introduced herself and said that they had come from Krakow.

"We live here in Warsaw," Eric replied.

"What is it like here?" asked Anna.

Eric tilted his head to one side as if he didn't understand the question. "It's fine, I guess."

"No, I mean ..." *How to explain this?* Anna took a deep breath and started again. "In Krakow, there have been some ... things that have happened. You know, Jews have been picked on and treated badly— even some of my friends." She wasn't ready to tell this boy about what had happened to her and Papa at the academy. "It's because of things like that that we want to leave—to go to Palestine with this new orchestra. That's why we're here. So I'm just wondering what it's been like in Warsaw."

A look of understanding passed over Eric's face. "Yes, of course, the same things are happening here. My friend was told to get off the tram because some passengers didn't want to ride next to a Jewish boy. He wanted to tell them to shove off, but he was afraid they'd gang up on him. So he got off and had to walk for miles." Eric paused and gestured around the room. "I imagine we're all here for the same reason. We all want to leave Poland."

"Do you know what our parents are going to have to do in this audition?"

Eric shrugged. "They're going to have to play like they've never played before."

Anna stared at Eric. There was something about him—the curiosity on his face, the honesty of his response. Anna needed a friend. Besides, he was the only person of her age who was there. So that already made him an ally.

"I know how we can sneak into the theater and listen to the auditions," Eric suddenly said.

"Pardon me?" Papa had told Anna that she would have to stay in the practice room. But Eric was offering her something that sounded like a better plan, something daring. Perhaps he wasn't as proper as she had thought.

"Are you game?" he asked.

The musicians were lining up, ready to go into the theater for their auditions. Papa signaled in Anna's direction, holding up his hand as if to tell her to wait there for him. She nodded and watched him go out the door. Then she turned back to Eric. "I'll follow you," she said.

Chapter 14

Eric led Anna out of the practice room, taking an abrupt right turn and leading her through a door that she hadn't even noticed. They descended a staircase and she found herself in a maze of passages and open doors, each one becoming narrower and darker. Anna felt a flicker of worry igniting inside, growing brighter with every turn into every hallway that Eric was taking. "Are you sure you know where you're going?" she asked, struggling to keep up.

"My father has played in this theater many times," he said over his shoulder. "This is how I get to watch him."

They continued turning this way and that until Anna felt as if they had just gone in a dozen circles and she had completely lost her sense of direction.

And just when she was regretting ever having agreed to go along, they suddenly emerged through a low archway to find themselves inside the grand theater. Well, they weren't actually inside the theater itself, at least not in the audience section. Eric had brought her to a small waiting area just to the side of the stage. From this vantage point, Anna could see the stage and she could see the audience, but when they crouched down as Eric instructed her to do, no one could see them. It was a perfect spot.

Eric nodded with satisfaction even before she could thank him. "I told you I knew where I was going," he whispered. She felt her face grow hot and knew it had turned to a color that was not unlike Eric's hair. But he continued as if he hadn't noticed. He pointed beyond the stage and out into the audience. Anna could see several men and women seated at a wooden table that had been set up across from some of the audience chairs.

Eric pointed to the man in the middle and mouthed the word "Huberman." But Anna couldn't see the maestro's face. He was sitting with his back to the stage. *How odd.* She raised her eyebrows to Eric as if to ask why. But he shook his head. He didn't seem to understand it either.

Anna continued to scope out the theater and

noticed that there was a large wooden board leaning on an easel that had been placed next to Mr. Huberman and his panel. She squinted to try to figure out what was on it and finally realized that it was a chart of an orchestra and it was divided into sections to represent the instruments: strings—that would be the violins, violas, cellos; brass—those were the trumpets and French horns; percussion—the drums and cymbals; and the woodwinds—clarinets, oboes, and the like. Under each section on the board, there were squares that seemed to indicate how many instruments there would be in that section. Several of the boxes were already covered with names. Anna didn't have to ask to know immediately what that meant. A number of musicians had already been chosen for those openings. Her eyes zeroed in on the woodwind section and on the clarinets. There were four boxes—four spots to fill. Two of the boxes were already covered with names.

Eric tapped her arm. A woman carrying a violin was walking onto the stage. She bowed in the direction of the panel. The man next to Mr. Huberman began to speak.

"Mr. Huberman will have his back turned while you are playing," the man began. "This is what we refer to as a blind audition. There will be no consideration as to your name or appearance. How you play will determine everything. You may begin at any time."

So that was it! Mr. Huberman would be picking his orchestra based only on how the musicians sounded to him. Anna wasn't sure if this was good or bad.

The woman onstage raised her violin to her shoulder, closed her eyes, and began to play, swaying slightly in time with the music. Anna could see Mr. Huberman's head moving from side to side. Every once in a while he stopped, placed his hand against his ear, listened, and then resumed his head nodding and swaying. The woman finished playing and bowed again. The man who had spoken in the beginning said, "Thank you. That is all." And the woman left the stage. Only then did Mr. Huberman turn around, and Anna finally had a chance to really see him.

He seemed to be an average-sized man, about as tall as Papa, and very formal looking in a gray suit with a high, stiff collar and a vest, from which he withdrew a pocket watch that he tapped on. He had slicked-back dark hair, a clean-shaven face, and eyes that were penetrating. But even from this distance, Anna could see that his face was kind, not severe or angry.

He began to talk with the men and women on his

right and left. With heads together, the group argued back and forth for what seemed like forever. Finally, Mr. Huberman jotted something on a slip of paper. The man who had given the instructions rose from his chair and placed this slip of paper over one of the spots on the orchestra chart. Anna squinted again. There was a name written on the paper and Anna knew immediately that it was the name of the violinist who had just played. That woman had made it into the orchestra. But Anna didn't have a moment to think about this when a man—this time carrying an oboe—walked onstage. And the whole process was repeated. Musician after musician walked on the stage, and Mr. Huberman had his back to them all. After each solo, someone simply said, "Thank you," and the musician was dismissed. Then Mr. Huberman would turn around and the debate would begin again.

Sometimes he wrote a name on one of his slips of paper; other times he wrote nothing. Once, he interrupted a cellist even before the musician had had a chance to finish. Another time he stopped a French horn player in the middle of her solo. Anna knew that wasn't good, and those musicians hurried offstage looking stunned and shaken.

When Eric's father came on, Eric stiffened next to her. His father raised his trumpet to his mouth and played. He made it through the whole piece. When he had finished and left the stage, Mr. Huberman had a long conversation with his colleagues, then wrote a name on the paper and posted it in the brass section of the chart. Eric grinned at Anna when he saw his father's name on the board, and she returned the smile.

Finally, it was Papa's turn. He walked onstage, bowed as all the musicians had done, listened to the instructions, and raised his clarinet to his lips. Anna moved slightly forward from her crouched position. Her heart was beating in big thumps like the timpani drum of an orchestra. And her breath was quick and shallow. She stared at her father and then out at the table where Mr. Huberman sat turned in his seat; she prayed and willed him to like what he heard. And when Papa began to play, Anna felt her heart soar with pride. This was her father, the renowned Avrum Hirsch, a great clarinetist. Anna had never doubted his talent and she had to believe that Mr. Huberman would recognize it as well. At one point, Eric put his arm on hers as if to stop her from leaping out onstage. She hadn't even realized that she was inching forward from her crouched position. If she wasn't careful, someone would see her.

Mr. Huberman did not interrupt Papa. When

her father finished playing, he bowed again and left. That was when Mr. Huberman turned and began the discussion with the other people at the table. Anna could feel the sweat begin to gather at the back of her neck. She was hot; she needed air and it felt as if the theater, enormous as it was, was closing in on her. What would Mr. Huberman do? Would he write her father's name down? Would he give them a chance to start a new life in a country far away from Poland?

The discussion seemed to be drawing to a close. This was it. Decision time. Anna inched forward again and held her breath. *Please choose Papa*, she prayed. *Please write his name down!*

"Hey, you little stage rats. What are you doing here?"

Anna and Eric reeled about and came face to face with an elderly man who had snuck up behind them. His face was badly scarred, and the lines around his cheeks and eyes were so deep that Anna thought they looked like the peaks and gullies of the hillside they had passed on the train ride to Warsaw. He held a broom in his thick hand, poised above his head. "No kids allowed. Get out of here!" He looked as if he might strike them at any second. Anna held her hands in front of her face, but before anything could happen, Eric grabbed her by the arm, pulled her out of her crouched position, and pushed her forward, back into the maze of hallways and arches and small doors leading away from the stage. "Run!" he whispered.

"Get back here so I can show you what we do to stage rats." The man was growling behind them but his voice was growing fainter and more distant as Eric urged her forward.

Anna turned and shouted over her shoulder. "No, wait. I have to go back."

"Forget it," Eric replied, huffing and puffing on her heels.

"But I didn't see if he wrote my father's name down."

"The only thing we would have seen is that broom coming down on our heads."

Hot tears were threatening to spill down Anna's cheeks. A voice inside her head was screaming. *Did he choose us? Did he save us?* There was no answer. Finally, they emerged into the musicians' waiting room just as Anna's father was entering.

Anna was still breathing heavily and her face must have been flushed. Papa touched her forehead. "Are you all right, Annichka? Do you have a fever?"

She shook her head, not trusting herself to

speak. She couldn't tell her father what she and Eric had done. He would have been terribly cross that she had disobeyed him and left the room to sneak behind the stage. But besides that, there was nothing to tell him, no way to reassure him about anything. They were both in the dark about what had just happened.

"Come, let's go home," her father said. "I think that went well."

Just as Anna was putting on her jacket, she felt a tap on her shoulder. She turned around to face Eric.

"I hope I see you in Palestine," he said, and then he turned and left the room with his father.

I hope so too!

CHAPTER 15

And then they waited. And waited. And waited. She had no idea when they might hear of the outcome of Papa's audition. She knew there were only two clarinet spots left in Mr. Huberman's orchestra. What if Papa hadn't been good enough for one of them? What if the answer was no? At one point, she had gone to search for Palestine in Papa's atlas, daring to imagine what it would be like to live there. It was a tiny country, especially when compared to Poland, and far away—across several countries and two seas, and nestled in between other countries, like Egypt, Syria, and Lebanon. There was so much that Anna would have to learn about this part of the world, if and when they ever got there.

In the meantime, there were more and more

newspaper reports about Jewish businesses that had been vandalized in Krakow and shopkeepers harassed. The last time Anna had walked by Mr. Kaplansky's store, she saw that it was closed and boarded up. She had no idea if he had been forced out or if he had decided to leave—like Renata and her family. The last radio report that Anna listened to had suggested that Hitler wanted to take over all of Poland.

"How can such a thing be happening?" Baba moaned. Papa didn't say a word.

More and more of Papa's students began to bow out of their lessons. Stefan arrived at her home one day to say that his family didn't want him walking on the streets in the evenings to Anna's place anymore. It was becoming too dangerous for a Jewish person to be out after dark. Besides, Stefan explained, money was scarcer these days since his father had been forced to leave his job. They could no longer afford the lessons. Papa shook Stefan's hand and wished him well, while Baba rushed to get him some cookies to take home to his family. Anna looked on and didn't say a word. Even though Stefan still sounded like a sheep when he played, it was hard to know that he would no longer be coming around for lessons. It was one more sign that things were getting worse in Krakow.

And then one day, Sabina, who played like sunshine, arrived to explain why she could no longer be one of Papa's students. He was surprised to see her when he opened the door.

"This is not your day for lessons, Sabina. But come in." He stood to one side of the door and motioned for Sabina to enter. She shook her head and stayed outside.

"My family just … umm … they just don't want it anymore," she said, stammering to get the words out.

"Are you going away?" Papa asked.

Sabina shook her head. "My father won't allow me to come here."

At that, Papa inhaled sharply and took a step backward. Sabina caught sight of Anna standing just behind her father. Sabina seemed nervous. In the presence of Anna's father, it seemed she had lost some of her boldness.

Anna's eyes narrowed. Why was Papa even surprised at Sabina's announcement? Anna wasn't. Sabina's father had stood watching Mr. Kaplansky being beaten. And then there were Sabina's repeated warnings that Jewish students wouldn't be allowed at school. She had even threatened that this day was going to come—when Papa would no longer have any students. Anna knew it would only be a matter of time before Constable Zabek would order his daughter to withdraw from lessons with her father. And here it was.

Papa had recovered by now. He stood tall and proud in front of Sabina and simply said, "Yes, I understand. I wish you well and I hope you continue to play the clarinet, Sabina. You have a gift."

Sabina didn't say a word. She turned and fled.

)(

One cold and wet day in January 1936, Anna arrived home from school. She shivered as she entered the house and brushed the snow off her jacket. She was longing for warm weather but she knew that it was still far away. And these days, the cold in Krakow stabbed at her cheeks and she had to bury her face in her scarf. The winter was so intense it made her wonder if spring would decide to skip a year. Papa was standing by the fireplace when she entered the living room. Baba was next to him. And between them on the mantle was a pale blue envelope. Without even asking, Anna knew what it was. The letter from Mr. Huberman had finally arrived.

"We waited for you," Papa began. "We didn't want to open it without you."

Anna nodded. "Okay," she said. "Go ahead."

Papa pushed his glasses up on his nose and reached for the envelope, holding it in hands that shook.

"Well, here we go," he finally said as he tore the envelope open and pulled out a single sheet of paper.

He read it through before looking up at Anna and Baba.

"What does it say, Papa?" Anna asked hoarsely. This was agonizing.

A slow smile began to spread across Papa's face, moving from the corners of his mouth and up to his eyes until his whole face was grinning. Finally, he whispered, "I'm in."

For a moment, no one moved. And then Anna bounded across the room, flying into her father's arms with a strength that nearly bowled him over. Baba was dancing around the room, flapping her apron above her face and looking more comical than Anna could ever remember.

"Read it, Papa," Anna shouted. "Read the letter out loud." She needed to hear the words spoken into the air before she would truly believe the news. The dancing and jumping and shouting finally stopped, and Papa, out of breath and still shaking, held the letter in front of him and read.

My Dear Mr. Hirsch,
It is with great pleasure that I am writing to you to invite you to become a member of the new Palestine Symphony Orchestra. I was truly impressed with

*your dazzling clarinet skills. Enclosed in this
envelope you will find your travel certificates,
which will enable you to leave Krakow on
April 20 and make your way here. Please make
your travel arrangements as quickly as possible.
I know this is a difficult time in your country
and in most countries across Europe. I look
forward to greeting you here in your
new homeland.*

*With gracious best wishes for safe travels,
Bronislaw Huberman*

"The certificates," Anna exclaimed. "Mr. Huberman
said they were enclosed." The certificates were the
most important part of this acceptance. They were
the keys that would allow Anna and her family to
leave Poland and be admitted into Palestine. Papa
reached into the envelope again and withdrew
another couple of official-looking documents. He
scanned them quickly and then paused. This time,
his face fell and his brow knitted together. He opened
the envelope a third time, shaking it upside down.

"What's the matter, Papa?" asked Anna. "The
certificates are there, aren't they?"

"There must be a mistake," Papa muttered,
continuing to search inside the envelope.

A sick feeling was rising up inside of Anna. But she was too afraid to ask what was wrong.

"What is it, Avrum?" Even Baba had stopped dancing.

Papa looked up, his face pale. "The travel certificates," he said. "There are only two of them. One for me and one for Anna."

CHAPTER 16

"It's a mistake!" Anna was the first one to break the silence. "He must have forgotten to add the third one for Baba. He knows about Baba." Baba was the one who had written the letter and signed her name at the bottom. How could Mr. Huberman not have included her?

"Of course he knows," replied Papa. "There are three members of this family, not two."

"Well then it's just a mistake, right, Papa?" said Anna.

"I don't know what to think." Papa was pacing now, holding the letter and two certificates in his hands as he walked in a circle. "Obviously, we can't leave here without Baba." He stopped suddenly and faced his family. "We won't leave here without Baba." He said this with a resolve that was unmistakable.

Baba placed her hands on her hips and pulled herself up as tall as she could. "What are you talking about?" she asked. Then she chuckled. "Did you really think that I would want to leave my home and travel halfway around the world? An old woman like me?"

What is she *talking about?* Of course Baba wanted to come with them. Anna stared at her grandmother and then at her father. What were they going to do?

"You go, and with my blessings," continued Baba. "I will stay right here where I've always been. And I will be fine."

Anna could not believe what she was hearing. Surely Papa wasn't going to agree to this.

For a moment, Papa did not reply. Finally, he pulled himself up, took a deep breath, and spoke in a voice that was calm and determined. "We go as a family, or we don't go at all. That's final," Papa added just as Baba was going to interrupt him again. "I will write to Mr. Huberman, explain the situation. If he is the compassionate man that I believe him to be, then I know he will do something for us."

With that, Papa turned and went into his study, closing the door behind him.

Anna wrapped her arms around her grandmother. "Papa's right, you know," she said, muffled in the folds of Baba's dress. "We can't go anywhere without you. You are the heart of this family."

Baba pulled Anna's arms away and blew noisily into a hanky that she withdrew from her pocket. "Okay, okay," she replied, trying to hide the tears that were already streaming down her cheeks. "It's enough now. I need to make you and your father something to eat."

Anna smiled weakly. Food was always the solution as far as Baba was concerned. "I'll help you," Anna said. But before following Baba into the kitchen, Anna walked over to her father's study door and tapped lightly.

"Come in."

Papa was hunched over his desk, ink pen in hand and scribbling furiously on a sheet of paper. He had not wasted any time in writing to Mr. Huberman. He didn't even look up when Anna entered.

She hesitated and shifted her weight from one foot to the other. Then she finally spoke up. "Papa?"

"Hmm?" He still did not raise his head from his writing.

She swallowed and started again, louder this time. "Do you think … I mean … would it help … if I also wrote a note to Mr. Huberman?" At that, Papa finally paused, laid his pen on the table, and gazed across the room at his daughter.

"I thought I would just explain to him how important it is for Baba to come with us. Do you think it would help?" Anna had seen the maestro's face in the audition room in Warsaw. She also believed that he was kind and compassionate.

Almost a full minute passed before Papa responded. And when he did, his voice was thick with emotion. "I think that would be a wonderful idea."

Anna disappeared into her bedroom and emerged a short time later. The note that she added to her father's letter was short and to the point.

Dear Mr. Huberman,
Thank you for accepting my father into your new
orchestra. You are saving our lives! My grandmother
wrote to you once before. But now, it is my turn to
write with an important request. Besides my father,
my grandmother is the most important person
in my life. I know you are very busy and very
important. And I know that many people are
trying to get out of Europe right now. But please
allow my baba to come with us to Palestine.
We cannot leave her behind.

Sincerely,
Anna Hirsch

CHAPTER 17

When a new letter arrived several weeks later, no one spoke as Papa tore open the envelope and scanned the contents. Anna was practically jumping out of her skin. *We will only go if Baba can go*, she thought. *Please make the news good.*

Papa closed his eyes and took a deep breath. Then he reached into the envelope once more and pulled out a single sheet of paper that he held above his head. "It's Baba's travel certificate," he said.

This time there was no dancing, no celebration, and no whoops of joy. Anna let out her breath, which she felt she had been holding for weeks. Everything suddenly felt lighter and fresher. Baba nodded and turned to go into the kitchen. From the living room, Anna and her father could hear sobbing—tears of relief.

Now that Papa had been accepted into the orchestra and they all had their certificates, Anna needed to learn more about the country that her family would be moving to. She pored over the newspaper, eager for every article that was written about Palestine. Not all the news was good. She discovered that the country was ruled by the British government. But the Arabs who lived there wanted their independence from Britain. They had been threatening to strike against the government for some time. But the other piece of news that Anna discovered was that the Arabs were also protesting against Jewish groups who wanted to create a homeland in Palestine. At first, Anna was confused by this.

"If Palestine is such a safe place for us to go, then why is there fighting between the Jews and the Arabs who are there?" she asked. She wondered if they were simply going to be trading one country of conflict for another one! That didn't make any sense.

Papa shook his head. "There are struggles everywhere in the world these days," he said. "But I know that Palestine will be safe for us. Don't forget how lucky we are to be able to go there."

Anna didn't question this any further. Yes, she had to remember that they were lucky to be getting out of Poland. Besides, she also read that Palestine was a place of deserts and the sea, and palm trees and camels—things she had never actually seen before except in pictures. What would it be like to live close to the sea and to be able to feel the sand oozing between her toes when she walked on the beach? The thought of that filled her with complete delight.

But there was little time left to think about much more. It was almost the end of March, and Anna and her family only had a few weeks left to pack up their belongings and get ready for this move. And there were still so many things that they needed to sort through.

"We will only be able to take what is absolutely necessary," Papa said. "The rest will just remain here in the house." They would be traveling by ship to Palestine. Their belongings were going to be boxed up and then placed in crates in the bottom of the ship. There was only a limited amount of space for all their things. And it was agonizing for Anna to try to decide what to take and what to leave behind. *This is exactly what Renata was struggling with*, Anna realized as she sat in the middle of her bedroom floor, legs crossed, trying to figure out what to bring with her. *Should I take my books?* she wondered. *And if so, which ones?* She loved them all and couldn't imagine leaving any behind. But choices had to be made. She also knew she couldn't take all of her pressed flowers. Not all of the frames would even fit into the suitcases and boxes. And the decision of which ones to pack and which ones to leave behind was just as painful.

"Just think, Annichka," Papa finally said as Anna sat amidst her collection. "You will begin to gather new flowers once we are in Palestine."

That was true, Anna thought. But leaving her treasures behind felt as if she were leaving bits of herself behind.

The easiest thing to pack was her clarinet. It was the first object that she placed on her "take" pile, making a mental note to remind Papa to put it in the safest possible place. It would be like taking a memory of her mother with her on this journey. Her clarinet would be packed along with Papa's, in a box also containing his music books and his collection of sheet music. He would need that to begin teaching students in Palestine, something he hoped to do once they got settled. Baba carefully packed her candlesticks that she lit every Friday night to usher in the Sabbath. But she cried over her favorite pots. She could only bring a couple of those along.

So many decisions! Take the bedsheets and the towels, but leave the crystal. It was too delicate and would probably break on the journey to Palestine. Take only clothing for warmer weather and leave the big winter coats behind. Palestine did not become as cold in winter as Poland did, which was something that Anna was definitely looking forward to. She would be happy to toss aside her big boots, heavy coat, and thick woolen scarves. Take the photo albums. They were precious and irreplaceable. But leave behind the paintings that adorned the walls of their home. And they were also leaving behind most of their furniture. They would acquire new beds, couches, and chairs once they figured out where they were living and how much space they would have.

Slowly but surely, the pile of belongings that would be coming with them grew like a mountain on the living room floor. Those items were packed in suitcases and boxes that were tied with thick strings to keep them secure for the journey. Anna's room began to look as if no one had ever lived in it.

Their date of departure was growing closer, and it was time for Anna to say good-bye to Stefan. She hadn't said anything to him about the possibility of her leaving. Papa had asked her not to say a word until a confirmation letter had arrived from Mr. Huberman. Stefan's face crumpled when she talked to him.

"I'm sorry," she whispered after blurting out the news.

"It's okay," Stefan replied, wiping his nose with the back of his hand. "It's just that I wish you weren't going." There were no jokes that day. Stefan's usual grin had disappeared.

She didn't know how to respond. It would have been a lie to say that she wished she weren't leaving either. Instead, she replied with what was truly in her heart. "I want you and your family to find a way to get out of here too."

Stefan lowered his head and shook it from side to side as he kicked aimlessly at the pavement with his foot. "I don't know if that's going to happen. My father doesn't seem to have any connections to get the papers we need to leave. Besides, he seems to think that all this will pass. I think we're going to stay here and wait it out." He looked up. "I hope you're going to write to me," he said. Anna nodded. "I don't even know how I'll be able to practice clarinet once you're gone," he added. "I know I don't sound very good, even though your father has always been so encouraging."

Anna felt tears gathering behind her eyes and she squeezed them tight. She knew she had to walk away fast or she would cry right in front of Stefan, and she didn't want to do that, didn't want to upset him any more. "Practice makes perfect," she whispered as she turned to go.

CHAPTER 18

Three weeks before their scheduled departure, Anna and her father were listening to the radio. Baba was in the background still moaning about her pots that she was leaving behind. Papa wanted to listen to a news report, but Anna was already worried about what they might hear. Lately, more and more speeches by Adolf Hitler were being broadcast on the radio. Anna shook every time she heard his voice spitting out hateful messages about Jews. But Papa insisted on turning the radio dial to the news. Anna was reading, doing her best to ignore what the announcer was saying, when he suddenly began to talk about Palestine. At that, she lowered her book and turned to the radio. Papa was already leaning forward in his chair. A nationwide strike had been called in Palestine. And that's when the worst possible announcement was made. All travel permits to that country were being frozen.

At first, Anna was confused about what that meant. She looked to Papa, who had removed his glasses. His brow was creased and his eyes were shut tight.

"I don't understand," she said. She knew there were problems in Palestine, but she hadn't realized things were so bad. This strike had put the country on high alert. The announcer was suggesting that even though Anna's family had their travel documents and even though they were scheduled to leave soon, Palestine would not allow them to enter.

"But it doesn't mean us, does it Papa?" she asked. Why was her father not answering her? He continued to sit in his chair, eyes closed. The announcer had moved on to another news item. But still, Papa did not move. Baba joined them in the sitting room. She had heard the report as well.

"Perhaps this restriction applies to others, but not to the musicians," Baba said weakly. "We have special passes from Mr. Huberman. Surely that means something?" She said this last part like a question, as if she didn't really believe it was true.

Anna felt that familiar pinch in her chest as the

air suddenly felt as if it were being sucked out of the room. The silence was thick and gloomy. Finally, Papa opened his eyes, replaced his glasses, and looked up at Anna and Baba.

"I don't know what to tell you," he said. "We will all have to wait and see what happens."

Then, on April 15, five days before they were scheduled to leave, a letter arrived from Mr. Huberman. In the intervening days, Anna had allowed herself to believe that everything would be fine. No news is good news, she told herself. They would be able to get out of Poland and no one would stop them. The letter from Mr. Huberman changed everything.

Dear Mr. Hirsch,
You have no doubt heard about the unrest
here in Palestine and the announcement that
permits have been halted. It is with deep regret
that I am forced to tell you that we must push
back the plans to have you and the other
musicians leave your country to join me here
in Palestine. I want to assure you that this delay
does not affect the creation of the orchestra.
It will simply have to wait a bit longer. I will
keep you informed of the plans and let you
know when another date has been chosen.

In the meantime, I wish you well and look
forward to the day when I will greet you here
in your new homeland.

My very best wishes,
Bronislaw Huberman

"Does he say how long the delay is for?" Anna asked.

Her father shook his head no.

"But do you think he's talking about days? Or weeks?" She didn't even ask if he possibly could have meant months. Or could it be years?

Again, Papa shook his head. "I read you everything, Annichka. That's all the letter says."

"But—"

"My darling, I have no more news for you. You know as much as I know."

Baba didn't say a word. Her eyes moved to the pile of luggage that sat in the middle of the room, almost waiting in anticipation for them to pick the pieces up and walk out the door. But within a few days of receiving Mr. Huberman's letter, the suitcases and boxes seemed to taunt them so much that finally Papa carried everything back into their respective bedrooms, where their clothes and belongings were returned to cupboards and drawers. And once again, Anna had so many more questions swirling through her brain. *When will we go? What will happen to us until then? Will we be safe?*

Papa had already resigned from his position at the academy. He had told everyone that he was leaving to take a position as a music teacher outside of the city, saying he wanted a simpler life. It was awkward to explain to the academy that the job in the country had fallen through. But luckily, Papa was able to convince the administrators to allow him to return to teach. At least that meant the family would have a small income to live on. There were no more students at home. No one was signing up for lessons at this time, and it made no sense for Papa to contact the ones he had already said good-bye to. Anna also returned to school. She didn't say much, even to Stefan. There really was nothing to say. And Stefan, sensing her discomfort, asked nothing. All he said was, "I'm glad you're still here. At least I've still got a friend in this class." Anna appreciated Stefan as well. But every fiber in her body was screaming to leave Krakow behind.

At home, the lightness seemed to have gone out of the family once more. They awoke in silence, went about their day, ate in silence, and then went to bed. Some evenings, they listened to the radio, but not to the newsreels. That was too depressing. And every time Adolf Hitler's voice filled the living room, Baba would bury her face in her apron and say, "Turn it off. I can't bear to hear him!" Papa would quickly change the station to a recording of classical music. That soothed everyone's frazzled nerves.

))(

The winter weather had finally left the city. When Anna walked to and from school, she could see the young children who had thrown off their coats to greet the warm sunshine that smiled down on the cobblestone streets of Krakow. The trams had their windows open, followed by horse-drawn carriages and mothers pushing baby prams. Shopkeepers brought their wares outside and placed them on wooden stalls, where everyone could stop and check them out. The streets smelled of smoked fish and sweet roasted peppers and rich, creamy cheeses. The citizens of Krakow emerged from hibernation and the city was alive and bustling.

At home, small buds had begun to appear on the flowers in the pots that Baba kept under the windowsills. Baba spoke to them every morning. "Good morning, beautiful tulip," she cooed. "It's so lovely to see you after this long, cold winter. Yes, my fine-looking daisy. You must try to grow big and strong." And the plants responded, pushing out of the dirt, higher and higher, as if they had heard Baba's voice encouraging them.

The sense of life and joy in the city was interrupted periodically by groups of soldiers who patrolled up and down the streets, marching with military precision. Anna hadn't seen the older boys from her school lately, but she sensed that they lurked somewhere, ready to pop out at any moment. She had taken to slowing down and peering around every curve and every building on the street, just in case danger was lurking around the corner. In fact, to Anna, the streets of Krakow felt more dangerous than ever. She felt that she was waiting for the next attack to happen, knowing it was a matter of *when* and not *if*. So she avoided going out except to school and to accompany Baba on her shopping excursions to the market.

Anna had received one letter from Renata in the months since her departure. It was long and newsy, and in it, Renata described her life in Copenhagen, the city in Denmark where they were living. Her family had found a small apartment and she was in a new school and impressing everyone with her math skills, which didn't surprise Anna in the least. She said that the people of Denmark and even the police were kind and friendly. And she ended the letter with these words:

I'm making some new friends, but no one as important as you. The framed poppy is on my wall and I look at it every day, hoping you are safe. We'll always be a team!

Anna had sobbed on her bed the day the letter arrived. As happy as she was for Renata, this was a stark reminder that her own family seemed no closer to leaving. She wondered if she was the only one in the entire city of Krakow who felt so miserable. She grew quiet, stopped talking most of the time. She had stopped asking Papa when they were going to leave. It only made him frustrated. He would rub his eyes with one hand while the other drummed furiously on the table. Anna knew he had no answer for her. And then Baba would start hovering over both of them and muttering under her breath, "Perhaps if you hadn't waited for the third travel document. You could have been gone by now." That always brought an emotional response from Papa. "Don't be ridiculous," he would choke. "We go as a family or not at all."

The only thing that brought Anna any peace was

when she practiced her clarinet. There was joy in the musical notes and in the melodies that filled their home. Even Papa seemed to relax when she played for him.

"That's beautiful, Annichka," he said one day as she finished playing a difficult passage. He wiped at his eyes and smiled at her. "You are becoming a real musician."

Anna sighed. It was high praise coming from her father. And she believed it was true. She no longer sounded like Anna the crow or one of the other barnyard animals. She sounded like the wind brushing against the treetops and the moon shining in the sky. But only she knew that the tune she was playing was also filled with notes that sung out a plea into the world. "When are we leaving?" her clarinet begged. "When will we feel safe?"

There didn't appear to be an answer.

CHAPTER 19

"Papa, Baba, it's here!"

It was August 1936, four months after the date they had been scheduled to leave. Anna had gone out to the mailbox as she did every morning, although lately, it had been with a kind of half-hearted, luke-warm enthusiasm. She would open the box, expecting nothing, and then, having that expectation fulfilled, she would close it up and go inside.

This morning had been no different. Baba had asked her to help with some baking and Anna was looking forward to shaping some yeasty dough into donuts, frying the shapes in deep oil, and then sprinkling them with icing sugar. The goal was to eat them when they were still warm. That's when the pastry would almost dissolve in her mouth.

She'd opened the box and was just about to close it up again when she saw the thin blue envelope shoved into the back. The handwriting on it was instantly recognizable. She grabbed the envelope, forgetting to shut the box, and ran back inside calling out for her father and grandmother.

Papa came running.

"It's his writing, isn't it?" Anna said, breathless.

Papa grabbed the envelope, looked up, and nodded.

"What are you waiting for?" Anna cried again as her father appeared to hesitate. And then she, too, stopped. This was the fourth time a letter had come from Mr. Huberman. Would this one be the lucky one? Or would there be more delays, more excuses, and more bad news?

Baba appeared from the kitchen. Her hands were covered in bits of sticky dough that she hadn't even bothered to wipe off. "Open it, my son," Baba said, holding her hands in the air like a surgeon about to operate on a patient. "Tell us what Mr. Huberman has written."

Papa looked one more time at his daughter and then at Baba, and finally, he tore open the envelope and extracted the letter. He read aloud without even looking ahead to see what was written. They would discover the news all together.

Dear Mr. Hirsch,
I am certain that you have been waiting for
news of your departure with some anxiety.
I must tell you that it has not been easy here.
The British government has continued to place
obstacle after obstacle in the way of Jews who
are trying to enter Palestine. But even the
head of our Jewish Agency, David Ben-Gurion,
has been reluctant to support my musicians,
wanting instead to save the precious permits
for farmers who could come here to develop
the land. There have been times when I
thought my lovely orchestra was at risk of
collapsing even before it had been formed.

Papa paused and took a handkerchief from his pocket to wipe the perspiration from his brow. Anna was practically jumping out of her skin. Papa finally replaced the hanky, readjusted his glasses, and continued reading.

I can now finally tell you that the approvals
have been granted from all those in authority.
Enclosed you will find your permanent new
travel certificates. Please make your travel
plans as quickly as possible, and I look forward

*to the first rehearsal of the orchestra in the
coming months.*

*With sincere good wishes,
Bronislaw Huberman*

*P.S. As previously agreed, you will find three
permits enclosed.*

With that, Papa reached into the envelope and
pulled out the three travel documents, holding them
high above his head as if they were trophies. Anna
grabbed the letter from Papa's hand to read it once
more. By the time she finished reading, Baba was
dancing around the living room, bits of dough and
flour flying off her fingers. Papa grabbed his clarinet
and accompanied her in a little jig. In between dancing, Baba kept spitting onto her fingers—"Puh, puh,
puh"—just in case there were any evil spirits still
lurking about. But this time, Anna wasn't worried.
She giggled at the ridiculous sight and then laughed
out loud, throwing her head back and roaring with
a force that came from deep within her. She couldn't
remember when she had last laughed like that. It was
as if all the uncertainty of the past few months had
been bottled up inside of her, ready to burst out in

this moment of celebration. There would be no more delays. They were finally going to leave.

The suitcases appeared once more on the living room floor, bulging with the things they would be taking with them to their new home. Anna added her pressed flower collection along with her precious clarinet to the pile, reminding Papa once more to put it in a safe place. And a couple of days later, Papa returned home with the tickets for their journey, paid for with the last of their savings. "And worth every penny," he exclaimed.

※

The day before their departure, Papa and Anna went to the Jewish cemetery to say their final good-byes to her mother. They passed through the big metal gate with the prominent Star of David on it at the entrance. Inside, they made their way through a winding path until they reached the spot where Anna's mother was buried.

Anna never minded coming here. It was peaceful. The sun played hide and seek in the branches of the huge pine trees that towered above the graves. Birds perched on the branches of the trees and chirped a soft melody to greet them. Anna gazed at the simple headstone on her mother's grave. It read

Here lies Miryem Frankel Hirsch
Loving wife and mother
Rest in peace

Several small stones had already been placed on top of Mama's headstone. Baba had been there earlier in the week, and some of the pebbles were still there from the last time Anna and her father had visited. The stones were a symbol that the memory of her mother's life would last forever, just like the stones themselves.

Anna and her father stood in a moment of silence. Then, her father spoke. "I know that there have been times in the last few months when I haven't been honest with you, or listened to you when you needed me to."

Anna stood absolutely still. Her father rarely spoke so personally, or so openly.

"I felt completely lost after your mother died," he continued. "But I think I'm beginning to find my way back."

"Papa, you don't have to say this," Anna began, but her father stopped her.

"Yes, Annichka, I think I do," he said. "And I vow to you that I will try to listen more closely to what you say, and be there for you when you need me."

Anna's heart swelled. "Do you think Mama knows we're going away?" she asked after another moment had passed.

Papa smiled. "Of course. And she will be with us on this journey. You believe that, don't you, Annichka?"

Anna nodded. "Do you think we'll ever come back?"

Papa paused. "That I cannot say."

Anna nodded again. "Shall I find another stone for Mama's grave?"

"Yes," replied Papa. "And find one for me to put on her headstone as well."

Anna walked around and found two small stones, which she and her father placed on top of the headstone. Once again, they stood in silence. And then, just before leaving, Anna reached into her pocket and extracted the dried red poppy that was part of her pressed flower collection. She had given one of these to Renata, but she knew she had to leave this one behind. Its place was here, watching over her mother. She placed the flower on her mother's headstone and then turned to leave.

"Good-bye, Mama," Anna whispered over her shoulder.

The sky was dark, and rain fell in fat puddles around their feet on the September day they left their home in Krakow. It was as if the city were weeping over their departure and begging them to stay. Anna knew that she would miss her friends, miss her house where Papa had taught clarinet lessons, miss her mother's grave. But beyond that, she was not sad to say good-bye to Krakow.

From Krakow they would travel by train to Genoa in Italy, before boarding the ship that would sail them to the port city of Haifa in Palestine. The train ride would take more than a day, and it was that first part of the journey that Anna and her family were dreading—a long and difficult route that would take them west through Germany before heading south to Italy.

Germany was the center of the storm, where Adolf
Hitler was promoting his hateful ideas, so many
of them directed toward Jewish people. Yes, they
had their precious travel documents with them. But
would that be enough to protect them as they passed
through that country? Anna hoped so.

She slept for much of the first part of the journey.
Her stomach felt strange. Just nerves, she told herself, like the time she had once performed for a few
of Papa's colleagues at the academy. Her stomach had
practically seized up then. A nap would calm her, and
help pass the time. They had a small compartment for
just the three of them, and the train lulled her to sleep
with its gentle rocking motion.

Once, she opened her eyes to see Baba standing over her, peering down. "Your face is hot, my
Annichka," Baba murmured as she pressed her lips to
Anna's forehead and laid her hand on Anna's cheek.
Anna shrugged the hand away and turned to look out
the window. Outside, the countryside of Poland sped
by. Over and over, Anna wondered if she would ever
see those rolling hills and green pastures again. She
whispered good-bye to each and every rock and tree
that they passed.

As they approached the German border, Papa appeared to grow more anxious. They were obviously

not going to be staying in Germany, but they would have to pass through border security in order to get to Italy. And that meant they would have to show their papers to the German authorities. Papa checked and double-checked the travel documents, making sure that the three certificates were there, names were spelled correctly, the dates were accurate, and everything was in order.

Once, he caught Anna staring at him and laughed. "You know how careful I tend to be about these things, Annichka," he said. "Everything is fine. No need to worry. It's just me being extra cautious. That's all."

He didn't fool Anna. She could see the sweat beading up on his forehead and his fingers twitching as he thumbed through the documents for what seemed like the millionth time. Baba was muttering to herself and spitting through her fingers, and her eyes darted from Papa to Anna and back again. The whole scene made Anna feel sick to her stomach. Or maybe she was already feeling that way. Whatever it was, the tension in the compartment was only adding to the sick feeling rising up inside of her. By the time the train came to the border, she thought she might throw up.

The train eased to a stop and steam hissed out of the engine as silence descended on Anna and her family. The three of them sat in their compartment for what felt like an eternity, saying nothing. Finally, they heard footsteps outside and the door to their train car was pushed open. A German soldier entered. He wore a brown army uniform with badges across his chest. He had a gun in the holster of his waist belt, and he wore tall, black boots that he clicked together as he came to attention. Anna's eyes were fixed on the bright red armband of his uniform, emblazoned with a black swastika, the symbol of Hitler's army. A second soldier waited outside the compartment. He wore a similar uniform, but on his head he had a helmet that looked like an upside-down pot that Baba had used to make stews.

"Papers!" the soldier demanded.

Anna shrank back and pressed against her father. Papa handed over the documents, and the soldier began to scan them.

"Where are you traveling?" the soldier asked.

"To Genoa," Papa replied. *He doesn't even sound nervous*, Anna marveled. His voice was calm and in control.

"And where will you be going from Genoa?"

That was the question that hung in the air. To reply that they were boarding a ship for Palestine would instantly identify them.

Papa hesitated for just a brief moment and then said, "We are sailing to Haifa."

"You are Jews," the soldier said.

"Yes," Papa replied.

There was a long pause before the soldier continued talking. "You're lucky you have these papers," he finally said. There was something sinister in his comment.

Up until that moment, the soldier had barely even looked at them. Now he looked up and his eyes moved across each of their faces, starting with Papa, then over to Baba, and finally coming to rest on Anna. She pulled even further back.

"The young one doesn't look well," the soldier said. "Are you feeling sick, kleine Mädchen?" He was calling her a little girl, and smiling when he said it. He leaned down until his face was just inches from Anna's. His breath smelled like cigarettes.

Anna was frozen with fear. Her heart was pounding so loud that she could barely hear what the soldier had asked, let alone respond. She couldn't even open her mouth to try. Her stomach, which had felt tense before, was now tumbling around inside of her, churning up in a way that made her feel lightheaded. Her father jumped in for her. "Perhaps she's just a little sick from the train ride. Nothing serious."

The soldier nodded. He continued to study each of their faces, looking back at their papers and then up again. Back and forth, up and down, for what felt like forever. Finally, he handed the papers back to Papa and turned to go. Just before leaving their compartment, he turned once more, snapped his boot heels together, and raised his arm in a salute to Adolf Hitler.

And then he was gone. It felt as if another full minute passed before Papa exhaled a slow and long breath. Baba looked up to the sky and closed her eyes. And that was when Anna did throw up, lurching forward and retching into the small trash can that Papa managed to grab and place in front of her in the nick of time. Anna hung her head for some minutes after that, still feeling her stomach heave and groan. Baba held her head until she finally leaned back, unclenched her jaw, and buried her face in her father's arm. The image of the soldier with his arm raised in that salute was seared in her mind. Within minutes, the train whistle blew and the train began to slowly chug its way out of the station. Anna barely looked out the window for the entire time that the train was passing through Germany. *The faster we get out of here, the better,* she thought. It took the better part of a day to get to the Italian border. Crossing through to Italy was not a problem, and after several more hours, the three of them finally arrived in Genoa, headed for the pier, and boarded the boat for Haifa.

As soon as they found their small cabin, Anna went straight to bed. Whether it was the soldier on the train or having thrown up, she felt terrible. Her head pounded, her stomach ached, and her cheeks burned. She wasn't even able to stand at the rail with all the other passengers as the ship slipped its moorings and sailed into the Tyrrhenian Sea. The journey to Haifa would take ten days, sailing the passengers south and around the tip of Cypress, then across the Mediterranean. Anna could hear the other passengers whooping and cheering. She longed to be next to them, but every time she tried to raise her head, the pounding began again, and she sank down deeper into the pillow and closed her eyes.

"Better to sleep, my darling." It was her father's voice. Or perhaps it was Baba. She wasn't sure. Maybe it was all a dream, and she would open her eyes and still be in her bed in Krakow, waiting for a letter to arrive from a famous violinist. Or maybe, just maybe, the next time she opened her eyes, they would be in Haifa.

CHAPTER 21

Anna didn't know how long she slept. The cabin grew dark, and then light, and then dark again. Every once in a while, she would open her eyes to find Baba standing over her, clucking and cooing and trying to force a few spoonfuls of hot soup down her throat. She turned her face away. Once, she awoke to find a doctor sitting next to her on the cot. At least, she thought he was a doctor. He had a stethoscope in his hand, which he pressed to her chest. There was a fuzzy image of Papa standing behind him. Papa's face was creased with worry lines.

Don't look so scared, Papa, she longed to say. But no words came out of her. She simply closed her eyes and drifted away again.

Another time, she awoke moaning. She had seen the soldier again, the one from the train. Had he followed them on to the boat? He was shouting in German, ordering her to get up and follow him. His arm with the swastika armband was still held high in the salute to Hitler. "No," she shouted. "No, I won't go. I have to stay here. Please don't make me go."

"Shhh, my darling." It was her father's voice, soothing her back to reality. "You're here with me and with Baba," he crooned. "Everything is okay. Just sleep, sleep."

She wanted to tell her father that the soldier was chasing her, but each time she tried to speak, he hushed her, and again she drifted away.

Then she dreamed she was in the audience of a great concert hall, listening to a group of musicians onstage. At first, the song they were playing was beautiful. But slowly, the musicians began to turn into barnyard animals and the sounds that filled the concert hall were the sounds of geese and ducks and cows. A man who looked like Mr. Huberman was standing on the stage shouting, "None of you are good enough to get into my orchestra!" *Make the horrible sounds stop,* her mind screamed. She pressed her hands to her ears, turned to the wall, and felt herself sleep once more.

Still another time, she dreamed about Mama, and a time when she'd taken Anna to see a puppet show at the Krakow Park. Anna was only five years old and she had become frightened at the sight of one of the puppets, which was dressed to look like a witch. It chased two smaller puppet children with a broom held high over its head. Anna had whimpered and clung to her mother, who calmed her and whispered in her ear. "Don't be frightened, Annichka. I'm here to protect you." Was that really the voice of her mother that she now heard in her dreams? Or was it still Papa stroking her forehead and telling her that she would be fine?

Finally, Anna woke to a bright beam of sunlight, filled with bits of dust particles, shining across her cot. It poured in from a porthole on one side of the small cabin. She hadn't even noticed the opening when they had arrived. *How many days ago was that?* She had no idea. But her mind felt fresh and clear. And when she pressed her hands to her face, her cheeks were cool.

"Well, hello!"

Anna rolled over to see Papa sitting in a small chair on the other side of the cabin. "It looks like you're back." He was smiling, a grin so big that it made Anna smile as well.

"How long have I been here?" she asked.

"Nearly four days!"

What! Had she really been sleeping for that long?

The journey was practically half over, and she hadn't even stepped foot outside the cabin!

"You've been quite sick, Annichka," Papa continued, noting the look of surprise on Anna's face. "Thank goodness there was a doctor on board. He gave you medicine that finally brought down the fever."

Yes, she remembered the doctor. But everything else was a blur.

"Where's Baba?"

At that, Papa smiled again. "Baba has not left your side, except to go and get food for you. That's where she is now. Every day, she's brought soup and toast here to the cabin, hoping you'd eat something. You've only had a couple of bites since we boarded. She will be thrilled to see you are finally awake."

As if on cue, the door to the cabin opened and Baba walked through. Her face exploded in a smile that seemed to stretch beyond her ears. "Annichka, I've brought you food."

Anna smiled again and struggled to sit up. She was weak after four days of being in bed. But she was also famished and the smell of the soup that Baba set in front of her was heavenly.

"Not quite like my cabbage soup from home." Baba sniffed. "But it will be fine and it will make you strong."

Anna tasted the hot liquid. *Delicious!* Baba urged her on, practically taking the spoon out of her hand and trying to feed her. It was all Anna could do to convince her grandmother to let her eat on her own. Finally, Baba went to sit on a chair at the foot of Anna's cot. But her eyes never left her granddaughter. Anna tried to finish the soup; she wanted to get it all in, if only to please Baba. But after several mouthfuls, she pushed the bowl away. She needed to get up, wanted to go out on the deck and see where they were and where they were going. She felt as if this voyage had slipped away from her in the last few days and she wanted to hang on to the last part of the journey. When she stood up, her legs felt wobbly beneath her and it took a moment before the room stopped spinning.

"Shall I come with you?" Papa asked after she had finished dressing. He stood close to her, brows still knitted together, as if he couldn't quite trust that she was fully recovered.

She shook her head. "I'll be fine, Papa. Besides, I can't go very far."

He seemed to accept that, but insisted that she put on a jacket. "It will protect you from the cool sea air," he said. Before going out the door, Anna checked herself in the mirror and pulled her long, unruly hair into two pigtails, which she quickly braided. Her face still looked pale, and she pinched her cheeks between her fingers to try to bring some color into them. Then she put on a jacket, waved good-bye to her father and grandmother, made her way to the deck, and walked over to the railing to watch the sea pass by.

Anna inhaled deeply as she looked out at the endless expanse of water. It smelled salty and a little fishy. But after four days of having been cooped up inside, she didn't care. She filled her lungs with the smell. A gust of wind brushed over her face, lifting strands of dark hair off her forehead. She wrapped her jacket tighter around her body and closed her eyes, feeling herself regain her footing as the ship bobbed gently underneath her.

The ship was called the *Fuga*. Anna had laughed when her father first told her the name. It was a funny-sounding word. "In Italian, it means escape," Papa said.

Now she whispered the word over and over in her mouth. *Fuga. Fuga.* It had become such a lovely word for a lovely ship.

Just then, she heard someone shouting and opened her eyes. A man standing close to her had lost his hat. The wind had picked it up and tossed it high into the sky. Anna watched as it sailed out across the sea and then landed on a wave. It bobbed there for a few seconds before it disappeared into the dark waters. The man was shouting as if he wanted it to fly back to him. But it was too late.

She closed her eyes again and took another breath, trying to block out the sounds of other passengers walking by and gulls squawking on the wind. Suddenly, someone touched her arm and she whirled around.

"I was hoping I'd see you here."

CHAPTER 22

"Eric!" she exclaimed. It was the boy from the audition in Warsaw.

He bowed in front of her and Anna recalled how formal he had been when she first met him. At least here on the ship, he wasn't wearing a suit. The wind blew his red hair straight up into the sky. He removed his glasses and squinted at her. "I heard that you were sick."

Anna nodded. "I'm feeling better now."

"So your father made it into the orchestra," Eric continued. "I'm glad."

"I guess it took longer for all of us to get out of Poland than we thought it would. But here we are." Anna swept her arms wide to the sea, and couldn't help but smile.

"You're happy?" Eric asked.

"Of course! Aren't you?"

Eric looked thoughtful. "I am," he said. "But I have to say that my mother is not as pleased to have left Warsaw. She thinks everything will be fine in Poland. She wanted to stay."

Anna nodded, wide-eyed. "My friend Stefan said the same thing! And even my father wasn't so sure about leaving at first."

"I think my mother is just afraid. She has no idea what's out there. None of us do, I guess." Eric looked out over the ocean as he said this. And then, a smile began to spread across his face and his eyes lit up. "I know where everything is on the ship. Do you want to explore it with me?"

Anna hesitated for a moment. The last time she had gone exploring with Eric they had very nearly been beaten by an angry janitor. Besides, her father had asked her not to be out too long. But it was so tempting to go with this boy. And she had already missed so much being sick in her cabin. She wanted to make up for lost time. And besides, she felt as if Eric might become a good friend. Now was the time to seal the friendship. She nodded and the two of them took off together.

The first stop was to the front of the ship. "It's

called the bow," Eric explained. "And those are the life boats." He pointed to a row of small dinghies suspended above the deck. "In case we capsize." Anna gulped. She knew it was possible for a ship this size to capsize. *Hopefully not this one!*

Next, he took her down a set of narrow stairs to another deck, where chairs were lined up side by side and a number of passengers were sunning themselves. "We can play shuffleboard over there," Eric explained, pointing to a few people with long poles who were pushing flat, weighted pucks across the deck.

From there, they moved inside, where Eric showed her the dining room, an echoing banquet hall larger than anything she had ever seen. Men in black waistcoats were moving about with linen and dishes. Eric and Anna tried to get into the kitchen—Eric swore he had done it the day before. But a rather large man appeared with a chef's hat and ordered them to leave. He brandished a soup ladle in the air like a sword. They wasted no time in turning around and bolting out of there.

Up some stairs and down some stairs, through some narrow passageways and under several arches, in one set of doors and out another. By the end of their exploration, Anna had no idea where they were. She had told her father that she couldn't go far, but she felt as if she had traveled around a small village. She was out of breath and her cheeks were red. But this time, it was with a healthy glow and not with the burn of a fever.

"Eric, wait," she called as her friend was about to head off down yet another set of stairs. "Stop. I think it's enough."

"But if we go down here, maybe we can get into the engine room. I was there yesterday."

Anna shook her head. "Maybe tomorrow. But I've got to get back to my room or my father is going to send out a search party."

Eric nodded. "Okay. Tomorrow I'll show you where the movie theater is."

Anna smiled. "I'll see you at dinner."

※

Anna gasped when she entered the dining room later that evening with her father and grandmother. When she had run through here earlier with Eric, it had looked big, but cold. Now, in the glow of giant chandeliers, the dining room was elegant and impressive. The tables were set with white tablecloths, silver forks and knives that gleamed, and crystal glasses. She felt as if she were a princess entering a castle ballroom.

"Has it been like this every night?" she asked,

wide-eyed. She still couldn't believe she had missed four full days of sailing.

"It has, my darling," Papa answered. "But I think it looks extra special tonight." Anna beamed with pleasure.

Papa held the chairs out for her and for Baba. She sat and looked around. Eric and his family were sitting across the room. She recognized his father from the audition. His mother, a nervous-looking woman with a pinched face, sat next to him. Eric had said that she wasn't happy to be leaving Poland. She looked like a woman who wouldn't enjoy much of anything. There was also a little girl at their table, and given her bright orange hair, Anna knew she had to be Eric's younger sister. Anna sat up in her chair, straining to catch his eye. When he finally looked across at her, she grinned and waved. He nodded and returned the greeting. Meanwhile Papa was pointing out other musicians in the room, famous instrumentalists who were to be part of the new orchestra as well. "That's Wolfgang Valk, and there's Jacob Mishori and Uri Toeplitz." Papa was breathless with excitement. The names meant nothing to Anna, but she was happy to see how animated her father was.

"There are more than seventy of us here, Annichka, plus all of our family members," he added. "From

Germany, Denmark, Hungary, Austria, and of course, Poland. There will be some local players from Palestine as well, but the majority of the musicians are like us, grateful to be leaving Europe at this time."

At each family table, there were children Anna's age, and older adults like Baba. Anna realized that Mr. Huberman had probably provided hundreds of extra travel certificates for these family members. *Fuga*, Anna thought again, repeating the name of the ship in her mind. She wondered if everyone knew how important and meaningful that name really was.

And then the food began to arrive, platters of baked chicken, and roasted potatoes, and cucumber salads. Baba sniffed suspiciously at each plate that was lowered to their table, and then nodded her approval. Anna began to eat, as though she were making up for a lifetime instead of just four days.

"Slow down, Annichka," Papa warned. But Anna barely heard him. She hadn't realized how hungry she was and each forkful seemed to restore some of her strength. Finally, there was no more room inside, and she laid her fork on the table and sat back. But the meal wasn't over yet. The waiters appeared once again, this time with plates of sweet crepes that were filled with nuts and dusted with icing sugar. When Baba tasted one, even she had to admit that they were as good, if not better, than the ones she used to make. Anna agreed. And even though she thought she might burst from all the food she had eaten, she managed to find a bit of space for the delicate dessert.

Papa was having his hot tea with lemon when the captain rose from his table at the head of the dining room and tapped on his water glass with a spoon. The passengers quieted down quickly and all eyes eagerly turned toward him.

"I think you will all agree that our chef has done another marvelous job of feeding us this evening."

Applause broke out across the hall as the chef entered from the kitchen. Several passengers rose to their feet. Others called out "Bravo!" and "Well done!" He was the same man who had chased Anna and Eric out of the dining room earlier that day, and Anna sunk down in her seat, just in case he saw her. She glanced across the room and noticed that Eric was doing the same thing. They needn't have worried. The chef was too busy bowing and acknowledging the ovation.

Then the captain clinked on his glass once more, and when the room had quieted, he continued. "In a few short days, we will be landing in Haifa, and I can't let this opportunity go by without asking if a few of you would give us a small concert. I know you're not really prepared for such a request at this time, but it would be an honor to hear you play."

In an instant the musicians in the room began to mutter and whisper, turning to one another and asking what music they had and what might be possible to perform. How could they turn down an invitation to play, especially when it came from the captain? And what an opportunity it would be to hear how they sounded playing together for the first time.

"What do you think, Annichka?" Papa asked. "Should I join the others? It's a celebration of sorts."

"Oh yes, please, Papa," Anna replied, her voice trembling.

Papa and the other musicians rose as one group and left the dining room to get their instruments. They all returned minutes later and began to tune up. And then, with a nod to one another, they raised their instruments and began to play. Even without a conductor, the sound was beautiful to Anna's ears. She closed her eyes and let the music wrap around her like a soft blanket. There were no barnyard animal sounds among these wonderful musicians. They played like fields of flowers and twinkling stars. They played like freedom.

CHAPTER 23

On the morning that the ship entered the harbor in Haifa, Anna was at the railing with all of the other passengers. There was no way she was going to miss the docking in the way she had missed the departure. The sky was clear blue and an intense sun shone down on her and the other passengers. The weather had been changing, growing warmer in the last days of the voyage. Here in the port of Haifa, the air was hot and dry.

"And it's only going to get hotter as the day goes on," Papa said.

The upper deck was packed with passengers all cheering and waving handkerchiefs as the city came into view. Anna cheered along with Papa, Baba, and everyone else. When she spotted Eric standing close by, she waved to him as well. In the last couple of days on board the ship, he had taken her to nearly every corner of the vessel. She felt she knew this boat almost as well as the captain did.

Eric waved back and then looked out at the sea. But when she followed his gaze, she was dismayed to see some boats with guns attached to their bows sitting in the water close by. The guns were aimed in the direction of their ship. She pulled on her father's arm and pointed toward the ships. Papa shielded his eyes in the glare of the morning sunlight as he looked out onto the water. A moment earlier, the cheers on board the ship had been booming. Now, the silence was nearly as deafening.

"Why are there guns?" a woman next to Anna asked.

"It's like the soldiers back home," another man added.

"Why are they here, Papa?" Anna asked.

Papa draped his arm protectively around Anna's shoulder and pulled her close to him. "I know that the British government has not been happy with the number of ships arriving from Europe with Jews on board. Some ships are being turned away. They're checking everyone to make sure our papers are in order."

Anna understood the importance of checking the

ships to see who was entering. *But why guns?* Guns meant something different. Guns were unfriendly. Guns meant *stay away.* This was not the welcome she had been expecting.

"But what if they turn us away?" she whispered. The thought of returning to Poland was horrifying.

"Please don't worry, Anna," Papa replied. "Our papers are good."

Anna stood close to her father as a group of officials from the British naval fleet boarded the *Fuga* to speak with the captain. Anna counted six of them, and they disappeared into the captain's cabin while the passengers remained at the railing, waiting to see what would happen. All eyes were trained on the doorway leading to where the meeting was taking place.

"How long do we have to wait?" Anna asked.

"The captain has all of our documents. And those British officials need to go through them. So this could take some time, Annichka. We must be patient."

Patient! Anna had patiently waited after Papa's audition to see if he got into the orchestra. She had been patient when they were uncertain about Baba's travel certificate. And then she patiently waited while the delay had been in place. She had had enough of being patient. Now she itched to get off the ship. She and the other passengers stood on the deck in silence as the minutes ticked by.

She wasn't sure how much time had passed, but suddenly, the party of British officials emerged from the captain's quarters and left the ship. Anna watched as the gunboat turned and headed back to shore. And at that very moment, the cheers on board the *Fuga* began again, building from a soft rumble to a joyous roar, rolling across the ship like a wave. Anna joined in, yelling and whooping at the top of her lungs. This time she knew they had made it.

It did not take long for the ship to dock. Anna, her family, and all the passengers disembarked, walking down the long platform to finally stand on the ground of Palestine. Anna's legs wobbled and it took a few minutes to adjust to not feeling the waves underneath her. Eventually, she got her footing and grabbed Baba's arm, afraid to lose her in the mass of people who were disembarking. Papa was just up ahead, pointing out their luggage to a man who was speaking in Hebrew, a language that was unfamiliar to all of them. Anna hoped they wouldn't leave anything behind. In all the commotion, it was nearly impossible to take in their surroundings.

"We have to get on the bus," Papa was urging. "There will be time to look around when we get to Tel

Aviv." That was where their new home awaited them.

Anna climbed onto one of the big buses that lined up for the passengers of the *Fuga*. Tires crunched on the stones underneath the bus as it revved its motor and pulled away from the port. They were on their way.

The bus traveled through a forested landscape snaking along a gravel road. The sun poked through the trees and shifted in the sky with every turn. And the canvas of colors in front of Anna's eyes turned from deep green to pale yellow to royal blue. There were a few buildings here and there by the side of the road and a couple of small villages that sprang up out of nowhere. But other than that, the area seemed pretty deserted.

Once, Anna grabbed her father's arm and shouted, "Camels, Papa! Look, there are camels!" Sure enough, the slow-moving beasts were traveling in caravans along the roadside, led by herders who carried long sticks and slapped at the back of the camels to keep them moving. At one point, Anna pulled down her window and stuck her head outside. The air was hot and sticky, and bits of dirt and grit clung to the inside of her nostrils as she inhaled. Her throat felt scratchy when she swallowed. But she didn't care. She kept the window open and her head outside for the remainder of the journey. Finally, after more time had passed, she began to see groves of citrus trees. Oranges and grapefruits hung low on the branches. She knew they had to be close to the city.

And suddenly, there it was. They had arrived in Tel Aviv. The paved streets here were busy with cars and bicycles and people walking briskly in the warm sunshine. British soldiers also marched on the streets. Papa had told Anna that tension between Palestinian Arabs and Jewish civilians was growing, and the army was there as a safeguard between the two groups, which were both claiming this land as their own. Anna shuddered. She didn't like the looks of the army. And the soldiers carried guns slung over their shoulders. It was a stark reminder that harmony in this part of the world was still far away.

Anna and her family climbed down from the bus, squinting in the afternoon sunlight. All the musicians had been assigned to live in a series of low-rise apartment buildings that were within walking distance of the Levant Fairground, where the orchestra would rehearse. Newly planted palm trees surrounded the area. Papa scanned the buildings and then smiled. "That's the one," he said, pointing ahead. All of the buildings were intensely white and spotlessly clean. It was all so different from the Old World splendor of Krakow, with its brown and black towering buildings and steeples.

The family climbed the stairs to the third floor and opened the door into a small apartment. Anna dropped the bag that she was carrying and ran from room to room, throwing open cupboard doors and exploring every corner of the place. It did not take long. The apartment had a small living room and dining room. There was a decent-sized kitchen. *Baba will be able to make all our favorites in here,* Anna thought. There were two bedrooms. She would be sharing one of them with Baba. But the best part was the balcony. It was almost the same size as the living room and partially shaded by a thick growth of vines that climbed up and over a wooded frame.

Anna ran to the railing and gazed out at the city. "Look, Papa," she shouted. "You can even see the sea from here." She had caught glimpses of it during the bus ride from Haifa.

Papa joined her on the terrace. "We will go there, Annichka," he said. "You will be able to swim in that sea."

"When?" she asked. "Can we go today?" Her family had vacationed by the Baltic Sea in Poland when Anna's mother was still alive. That had been such a long time ago.

Papa laughed. "No, my darling, not today. But soon," he added when Anna's face fell. "First we must go down to the concert hall. Mr. Huberman will be speaking to all of us this afternoon." At that, Anna's face quickly brightened. "Come, let's freshen up," he said. "We don't want to be late for this first gathering of the orchestra."

A short time later, they were seated in the concert hall waiting for Mr. Huberman to take the stage. "Concert hall" was a generous description of the space. It was a work in progress. The floors were unfinished wood. So were the walls. And the ceiling was a simple tin covering. There were workmen and carpenters everywhere, pounding nails into the floor and walls. Sawdust flew across the room like the sand blowing across the desert.

Everyone from the ship was there, along with other musicians whom she didn't recognize. Papa and most of the men were still wearing suits, but the women were wearing light dresses and the boys were in open-necked shirts. Baba was fanning herself, trying to stay cool in the overheated building. Anna couldn't see Eric in the crowd, but she was sure he had to be there. Nervous and excited chatter competed with the pounding of the workers' tools. She should have been exhausted after the long journey and her recent illness. But she felt more alive and alert and excited than she could ever remember.

Suddenly, there was a hush. Anna looked up.

Bronislaw Huberman walked across the stage and approached a microphone that had been set up for him. He gazed out at them all. When Anna had seen him at the audition in Warsaw, he had looked so serious, focused on every musician who entered the theater and on what they were playing. Here, on the stage of this newly forming concert hall, he was still quite formal looking, in a three-piece suit and tie. But he looked relaxed, even happy. Anna stared, her mouth open. This was the man who had written her father's name on that slip of paper that ensured her family would be able to get out of Poland. He was the man who had sent the travel documents—even the extra one for Baba. Not only was he a great musician, as Papa had repeatedly told her, he was a rescuer. And for that, she and her family owed him more than they would ever be able to repay. Anna inched forward in her seat.

He smiled at them all, raising both hands above his head and grasping them together as if he were cheering for them. "I welcome you all to Palestine," he began. "I know this journey has been a long one for you. But the journey is over. You are all here. You are all safe."

At that, the audience erupted in spontaneous applause. No one clapped louder or longer than Anna.

Finally, Mr. Huberman raised his hand to hush the crowd. "We will begin rehearsals tomorrow," he continued. Murmurs broke out among the audience members, and Mr. Huberman raised his hands once more. "Yes, tomorrow. We are scheduled to give our first concert in December—only a few months away." More murmurs and another silencing hand from Mr. Huberman. "And I have great news for all of you. That first concert, the first introduction of the Palestine Symphony Orchestra, will be conducted by none other than the greatest maestro of our time, Arturo Toscanini."

Anna thought Papa was going to fly out of his chair at this news. Along with everyone else, he was cheering and clapping so loud. He looked as if someone had just given him the best birthday gift. Even Anna knew who Toscanini was. She and her father had listened on the radio to concerts conducted by Toscanini, who came from Italy but conducted all around the world. Each time, Papa would close his eyes and say, "Listen, Anna. He demands perfection from his orchestra and they give it to him."

The cheering went on and on, and Mr. Hubeman could do nothing to quiet them. Finally, he just laughed and waved, and walked off the stage.

Before heading back to their apartment, Anna

caught up with Eric, whom she finally managed to find in the crowd. He looked more relaxed in his shirt with the sleeves rolled up to the elbows.

"We're living in the building next to yours," he said. *How does he always manage to discover these things so quickly?* "We'll go and explore the city."

Anna smiled and nodded. She had to unpack. They had to get settled. And tomorrow, she would be starting school while her father was in rehearsals. But yes, exploring the city with Eric was definitely on her list of things to do.

CHAPTER 24

Papa distributed the suitcases and they got to work unpacking. Anna mentally divided up the room she was going to be sharing with Baba, being careful to make sure there was equal space for both of them. She quickly unpacked her clothes and her books. Once those things were put away, she placed several of the framed flowers from her pressed flower collection on the wall on her side of the room and stood back to admire them. *Perfect!* They immediately brightened up the white walls. While Anna was putting away her things, Papa was busy with his books. Baba was rummaging through the kitchen and muttering to herself. "I should have brought my soup pot. How will I feed this family without my soup pot?"

Slowly but surely, everything was finding its place.

But when Anna went to look for her clarinet, she couldn't find it.

"Papa," she called as she searched through the boxes, "I don't see my clarinet. Do you know where it is?"

He looked up from the pile of sheet music that he was sorting. "No, I don't. But I'm certain it must be here."

Anna continued going through the boxes. "I know it was there when we were packing. Remember, I put it on the pile with my special things?" Her pressed flowers had arrived safely, but where was her clarinet? "I don't remember if it was there when we got on the ship," she added. The truth was, she had been so sick after the train ride that she couldn't remember much about what they had brought on board. Now, the same sick feeling was beginning to build from deep inside her. Her clarinet! The gift from her mother. Her prized possession! It couldn't have gotten lost, could it?

"Don't panic," said Papa as Anna darted from room to room. "There are still a couple of boxes out on the balcony that we haven't emptied yet. Perhaps it's in one of them." Anna ran out the screen door and dove into the last of the boxes, throwing the contents about the terrace and digging down toward the bottom. When they were empty, she looked up. *Nothing!*

How could this be? She was feeling sicker by the minute. Papa was trying to stay optimistic. "I'm sure it will turn up," he said. "Perhaps the ship will locate it and send it here, or it will turn up at the port in Haifa. In the meantime, you can practice with mine."

Normally that would have brought a smile to Anna's face. Papa rarely let anyone touch his clarinet and this would have felt like quite an honor. But in this moment, his offer did little to make her feel better. Anna didn't reply. She walked into her new bedroom and looked around, feeling lost and alone. And then, she sank down onto the floor, buried her face in her hands, and sobbed. Baba hovered like a hummingbird. Papa had nothing more to say that might comfort her.

Anna cried and cried, letting the tears wash down her face like a warm spring rain. She cried for her home left behind, and her mother who was gone, and her friends who had disappeared. And she cried for her beautiful clarinet that was either on a train in Germany, or on a ship in the middle of the sea, or perhaps even overboard and on the bottom of the ocean, like that man's hat that had flown off his head. Wherever it was, it was lost to her. When Anna finally went to bed later that evening, she turned her face away from Baba, not wanting to talk. And when she awoke in the morning, she was still quiet and distant.

Papa kissed her good-bye before leaving for the concert hall and his first rehearsal. "Please try to be happy, Annichka," he said.

Anna gulped and tried to smile for her father. She did the same for Baba, who was still hanging close by and watching every move that Anna made. "I'm okay, Baba," Anna said. "Really, I am." Baba didn't look as if she were convinced, but she finally backed away and allowed Anna to get ready for school.

It was raining that morning. Anna made her way down the hill from the apartment to a small clapboard building where she would be studying along with the other children of the musicians in the orchestra. They were going to learn Hebrew, the language of this country. And once they were reasonably fluent, they would enter a regular school with local children.

The ground was slick with mud, and she slipped and slid all the way there. The rain didn't help to lift her spirits. But she had to admit that she was at least somewhat curious about this new school. Most of all, she was looking forward to seeing Eric again—her friend! She entered the small room and found a seat next to him. He nodded understandingly when Anna whispered to him about her lost clarinet.

"I lost my trumpet once," he said. "But someone found it and returned it to me."

"I don't think anyone is going to return my clarinet."

"Maybe you'll get a new one."

Anna shook her head. "Not any time soon. It's too much money."

Even though the musicians would be paid a modest salary to be in the orchestra, Papa wouldn't be teaching for quite a while. He would also need to learn Hebrew before he could offer lessons to students. And Anna knew that so much of their money had been spent in just getting here. There wasn't much left over for an expensive clarinet. She didn't want to think about it anymore. The sadness was too overwhelming. So instead, she tried to focus on the Hebrew lessons. But that didn't make her feel much better. The language was difficult and made trickier by the fact that the written letters didn't look anything like any letters she had ever seen before. Hebrew script had wiggles and dots and marks and lines that were meaningless to her. At the end of the

first hour of trying to copy an exercise into her work-
book, Anna was so frustrated that she laid her head
on her desk and closed her eyes.

"Don't be so hard on yourself."

She looked up into the sympathetic eyes of Mrs.
Rose, their teacher. Mrs. Rose had a face that was as
soft and as round as her body, with eyes the shape of
almonds and short, curly hair the color of sand. She
was barely taller than any of the children in the class.
She reminded Anna of Baba. Any minute now, Anna
expected that she would pull a cake out from behind
her back and offer it to her. But more than anything,
Anna loved her name, a reminder of her collection of
dried flowers.

"I don't understand anything," Anna moaned.

"Not yet. But you will." Mrs. Rose wore her glasses
so low on her nose that Anna was tempted to reach
out and push them up. "You'll see," the teacher continued. "You will be talking like a *sabra* in no time."

"A what?"

"It refers to a rather ugly cactus plant from the
desert with sharp thorns on the outside. But the plant
has a soft and sweet pulp under those thorns. Here,
we use the expression to refer to a Jewish person born
in Israel; someone who is tough on the outside, but
soft on the inside."

Anna wasn't sure if she would ever feel like a *sabra*. She counted the minutes until the class ended. Then she packed up her books and headed out the door with Eric.

CHAPTER
25

"Follow me," he shouted. "I know a shortcut to the rehearsal hall."

Once again, Anna had no time to wonder how he had learned about that in such a short time. She picked up her pace and followed Eric down a set of stairs, under a fence, and across an open field. The ground was getting muddier and slipperier from the rain that continued to fall. It was all Anna could do to keep up with Eric and stay upright.

Finally, they arrived at the concert hall and pushed open the door. Before entering, Anna paused and tried as hard as she could to wipe the mud off her boots. But in the end, it didn't really matter. The unfinished wood floor was already covered in dirt and mud from the carpenters who were still there working on the construction of the hall. Inside, there was an overwhelming smell of paint and turpentine. Anna wrinkled her nose but didn't have a chance to say anything to Eric. He motioned her to follow him to a spot to the left of the stage. From there, Anna had a full view of the members of the orchestra, including her father.

Mr. Huberman was onstage, poised in front of the conductor's stand with his arms raised and a baton in his right hand. He had removed his formal jacket and vest, and the sleeves of his shirt were rolled up above his elbows. "Again, please," he ordered. "From the beginning of the second page."

He counted out a few quick beats and then brought his baton up to signal the musicians to begin. But with the sound of the steady rain that was pounding on the tin roof, it was nearly impossible to hear anything. The rain was louder than the drums. On top of that, some water was leaking into the concert hall and dripping onto the musicians. One of the violinists jumped out of her seat as a trickle of water became a stream that poured down onto her. "I cannot play like this," she moaned. Others chimed in to agree.

Finally, Mr. Huberman laid his baton down on the stand. "It looks as if we will have to adjourn for the day," he said, rolling the sleeves of his shirt down to his wrists. "There are many things I can control. But the weather is not one of them. Enjoy the rest of your day, ladies and gentlemen. I will see you all back here bright and early tomorrow morning. And let us hope that the rain has stopped by then."

The musicians rose and began to put their instruments back into their cases. Eric ran off to speak to his father. Anna didn't even notice Mr. Huberman approaching until he was standing next to her.

"I saw you and your young friend come into the hall," he said.

"Oh, I'm sorry. Are we not allowed to be here?" She was horrified that she might have broken some kind of rule about who could and couldn't come to the rehearsals. *Why didn't Eric warn me about that?*

"Of course, you are welcome to be here. I'm just sorry we couldn't provide a better rehearsal for you to hear."

She smiled at him, suddenly shy and uncertain of what to say.

"I don't think we have been introduced." He bowed formally. "I am Bronislaw Huberman."

Anna stood and curtsied. "My name is Anna Hirsch. My father is Avrum Hirsch." She pointed. "Clarinet."

"Of course. You are the young lady who wrote to me on behalf of your grandmother."

He remembers that! "And thank you for everything you've done for my family," Anna blurted out. "If it wasn't for you ..." She didn't even know how to finish the sentence.

Mr. Huberman brushed aside the comment. "And do you also play the clarinet, Miss Hirsch?"

Anna sighed. "My father has been teaching me. But my clarinet got lost." She explained about having been sick on the boat and only discovering the missing clarinet when they were unpacking. "I have no idea what happened to it."

"Oh, that's a pity. You must be terribly sad about that."

Anna nodded. She lowered her eyes to the ground, blinking furiously, afraid she might start to cry in front of Mr. Huberman.

"But I know the feeling," he continued. "My violin has also become lost."

At that, Anna looked up, wide-eyed. "It has? Where did you lose yours?"

"In America, while I was there for a concert." He leaned forward and whispered, "I believe someone may have taken it."

"Oh no!" she exclaimed. "I'm so sorry."

"And I'm sorry that yours is also missing. Perhaps we will find our lost instruments one day."

"I hope so." She said that half-heartedly, as if she didn't believe it was possible.

"Well, it was a pleasure to meet you, Miss Hirsch. Please come back to the rehearsal hall any time you wish."

And with that, he turned and walked away.

CHAPTER 26

Walking home with Papa after rehearsal, Anna told him about her conversation with Mr. Huberman.

"He told me that I could come any time to listen to the rehearsals," Anna explained. "That's okay, isn't it, Papa? Mr. Huberman said it would be okay."

Papa looked at her thoughtfully. "And will it make you happy to come here to watch us rehearse?"

Anna nodded eagerly. "Oh yes, it will!" It would be just like the times she had gone to the academy to listen to her father rehearse—before he had been moved to the ghetto chairs.

"Then I think that is exactly what you should do," Papa said. "As long as you get your schoolwork done, you are welcome here any time."

Over the next few weeks, Anna took Papa's message

to heart. She worked hard at school every morning. And although the Hebrew language was still frustrating at times, even she had to admit that she was beginning to learn more words and phrases. And the squiggly letters were starting to make sense. Some days, Baba would drag her to the market to help negotiate the price of a chicken or some vegetables for the new soup pot that she had finally purchased. It wasn't that Baba was not capable of haggling. She had bargained with the vendors back in Krakow like a pro. But Baba was not having any luck mastering Hebrew and needed Anna there to help.

The open-air market in Tel Aviv was at least twice or maybe three times the size of the one in Krakow, and it pulsed with activity. Hundreds of stalls displayed everything from poultry to cheese to vegetables and even fabrics and furniture and handicrafts. Anna inhaled the rich smell of spices like paprika, turmeric, and cumin, and the strong aroma of black coffee. The vendors shouted at passersby to stop and examine their goods. Everyone bartered for the best price.

"Five shekels for a chicken that size?" Anna argued in Hebrew with the butcher. "That's ridiculous. My grandmother won't give you more than three." It pleased Anna that she was able to negotiate with the merchants. She was on her way to sounding as fluent as one of the *sabras* that Mrs. Rose had mentioned on the first day of school.

To help improve her Hebrew even more, she stayed after school once a week to do homework with Eric. Between the two of them, it was often easier to figure out the difficult Hebrew script.

"I think this says, 'I am looking for a doctor,'" Eric said one afternoon as they sat translating a passage.

Anna laughed out loud. "You're going to have a big problem if you think you'll find a doctor saying that! It actually says, 'I am looking for a bathroom.'"

Eric grinned. "Okay, I won't say that if I'm sick. Though it might also help in that case!"

Anna was learning more and more about her new friend during these times together. Like Anna, Eric had learned to play trumpet from his father beginning at a young age.

"My father sounds much stricter than yours," Eric told her. "He's not the easiest person to talk to."

Anna recalled how stern he had looked when she spotted him at the audition in Warsaw. "And your mother? Is she getting used to living here yet?"

At that, Eric looked away. "Not really. She isn't saying very much, but I can tell." He paused before continuing. "She thinks the troubles here are almost as bad as the troubles back in Poland."

Anna recalled that Papa had warned her of the growing tension between Palestinian Arabs and Jewish refugees. He didn't want her to be out on the streets alone, except for going to school and to the concert hall, or if she was out with him or with Baba. When Anna asked why there was such conflict between the two groups, Papa tried to explain that the Arabs felt threatened by the British authority and also by the arrival of so many Jewish immigrants, whom they saw as trying to take over their land.

"Are they threatened by us?" Anna asked.

Papa nodded sadly. "There is one piece of land here and several groups of people who want it. It's not the same as in Poland," he added when he saw Anna's stricken face. "But it's still a difficult time here. We just have to be careful, that's all."

Anna told Eric what Papa had said, and added, "Maybe you can talk to your mother and tell her that the troubles here are not the same as those back there."

Eric shook his head. "I used to be able to talk to her more. But she's been so nervous lately, and quiet—like she's disappeared even though she's standing in front of me. She never used to be like that."

Anna nodded sympathetically. "My father was like that when my mother died—quiet and even angry. But he's come out of that now."

"I keep thinking that one morning my mother will wake up and feel better and realize that we made the right decision to come here," Eric continued. "But so far, I'm still waiting."

"Are *you* glad you're here in Palestine?" Anna asked.

Eric nodded. "Yes."

"Then that's the most important thing. Hopefully your mother will come around and see it that way too. I'm happy you're here," she added. And saying that, Anna realized that she was beginning to feel at home in this new country.

Most days, after her schoolwork was done, Anna eagerly made her way to the concert hall to listen in on the rehearsals for the first concert, which was only a couple of months away. Flyers had already been posted throughout the city. The radio blared advertisements for the new Palestine Symphony Orchestra and for their inaugural concert—and for the appearance of maestro Arturo Toscanini as its conductor. All the great dignitaries from across Palestine would attend. The concert was even going to be broadcast on the radio worldwide. Papa said that more than one hundred thousand people wanted seats in the concert hall, but there were only two thousand tickets. It would be impossible to accommodate everyone.

Today, the orchestra was rehearsing a long four-part symphony written by the composer Johannes

Brahms. The last part of that symphony was Anna's favorite. It was so loud and dramatic that it made her heart beat wildly, especially at the end, when all of the instruments joined together. Often, when the musicians would lay their instruments down, Anna realized she was sweating almost as much as they were from the energy she exerted just listening and holding her breath.

While the orchestra was taking a short break, Mr. Huberman came over to say hello. "How are we sounding today, Miss Hirsch?"

"Wonderful," she replied, breathless. They always sounded wonderful to her.

"Any luck locating your clarinet?"

She shook her head. "What about your violin?"

At that, he sighed. "I think it may be lost forever."

Anna frowned. "But if you don't have a violin, then what will you play for the concert?"

A slow smile began to spread across Mr. Huberman's face. "I have decided that I won't be joining the orchestra this time."

Anna wasn't sure she understood this. Mr. Huberman was a great violinist. And this orchestra was his creation. Why would he not want to be part of its historic opening concert?

"It's not because of my violin," he added quickly.

"I just want to sit in the audience and enjoy the music along with everyone else."

The break ended, and the musicians gathered in their spots onstage once more. Mr. Huberman excused himself to go back to the conductor's stand. As he walked away, Anna looked around and wondered if the hall would be finished in time for the concert.

She watched the workers pounding nails into the floor and walls. The racket was so loud that the newly constructed walls were practically vibrating. And it was not the first time that this had happened. There had already been several days when Mr. Huberman had had to abandon the rehearsal because no one could hear over the noise. This afternoon was no exception. Mr. Huberman was having the orchestra work through a particularly difficult passage in their symphony. The music needed to be soft at times and then build to a great crescendo. But the softness of the violins was completely drowned out by a symphony of hammers that all went to work at the same time. A moment later, the pounding and hammering reached an all-time high. Mr. Huberman brought his baton to his side and the orchestra members lowered their instruments. He turned slowly to face the construction workers. From where Anna was sitting, it looked as if the maestro had had enough of all of this noise.

He stood for a moment, hands clasped behind his back, head lowered. Anna could see that he was breathing deeply, either trying to calm himself or building up to an outburst. The musicians were also staring at him, and now they glanced at one another, wondering what was going to happen next. Minutes passed. Anna waited and watched. Mr. Huberman remained standing onstage but his face was growing redder with each passing second. Finally, he walked offstage and over to where the carpenters were still banging and drilling.

"Excuse me," he said in a loud voice.

The workers did not hear him. They continued with their construction.

"Excuse me!" This time he shouted the words.

The workers stopped suddenly, hammers still held high in the air. The silence in the concert hall was a welcome relief.

Mr. Huberman pulled himself up to his greatest height. "We cannot continue with these rehearsals if you continue making that horrible noise," he said.

The workers stared at one another and at Mr. Huberman. Finally, one of them stepped forward, wiping his paint-splattered hands on his overalls. "I'm sorry, maestro," he said. "But we have our work to do and we don't have much time to finish."

"But we must rehearse," Mr. Huberman sputtered.

The worker shrugged. "You have your work to do, and we have ours."

From where Anna was sitting, it looked as if Mr. Huberman might explode. His hands were shaking, his nostrils flared, and his face was as purple as the eggplant Baba had bought at the market the previous day. Finally, he asked in a voice that was steely cold. "How much money will you charge to do this construction at night?"

At first, no one responded. Then the workers gathered in a circle and began to talk among themselves. Anna watched in amazement. Mr. Huberman held his ground, waiting with his hands clasped tightly behind his back. Finally, one of the workers, the same one who had spoken earlier, stepped forward again.

"Maestro," he said. "We will do this work at night, as you have requested. But we do not want extra payment for our work. What we would like instead is for you to promise that we will all have tickets for the first concert in December."

Mr. Huberman stared at the workers and they stared back at him. Finally, he replied, "Done!"

It was the first day that Maestro Arturo Toscanini was going to be present at a rehearsal of the orchestra. He had arrived the night before from Italy. Everyone thought he might need a couple of days to rest. But he had let it be known that he wanted to hear the orchestra first thing in the morning. That morning, Anna's father paced around the apartment like it was the first day of school.

"Baba," he shouted, "where are my cufflinks? I can't wear this shirt without my cufflinks!"

Baba appeared from the kitchen, shaking her head. "They are on your sleeves." Sure enough, the cufflinks were dangling from the ends of Papa's shirtsleeves.

A moment later, Papa shouted, "My music. It's disappeared. Where is my music?"

This time, Anna stepped forward. "It's all ready for you at the door. Don't you remember, Papa? You put it there last night so you wouldn't forget it."

"Well, just make sure no one touches it." He turned around, mumbling under his breath. "Where did I put my clarinet?"

Anna showed him that his clarinet was also at the front door. If the tension in the air weren't so thick, Anna would have burst out laughing. It was comical to see her father, usually so composed, running around the apartment.

"If your head wasn't attached to your neck, you wouldn't know where it was, either," Baba muttered as she stepped out of Papa's way and returned to the safety of her kitchen.

Finally, Papa was ready to go. Anna inspected him and adjusted his tie. "Don't be nervous, Papa," she instructed. "You always tell me that everything will be fine. So I'm telling you that as well."

Papa paused and took a deep breath. "You are growing up in front of my eyes, Annichka. And more and more like your mother." He paused, eyes far away, and then resumed talking. "Yes, I will try not to shake too much in front of Maestro Toscanini." Then he leaned forward and smiled. "It wouldn't do my playing any good, would it?" He paused for another moment, deep in thought. "Do you know that Toscanini once refused to conduct a concert in Germany because he hated everything that Hitler was doing there? He must be such a compassionate man." Then he looked once more at Anna. "Will you come to watch the rehearsal this afternoon?" he asked.

Anna nodded. "I wouldn't miss it for anything." She kissed her father on the cheek as he scurried out the door.

Her Hebrew lessons that morning seemed to drag on forever. And her mind was everywhere except on the work. She couldn't conjugate her verbs, forgot her spelling words, and mispronounced some simple sentences. At one point, she even forgot her teacher's name and stared at her blankly when Mrs. Rose called on her to answer a question. Finally, her teacher took her aside.

"What is wrong with you today, Anna?" Mrs. Rose asked. "You look as if you are in another world."

Anna explained that the great conductor Toscanini was going to conduct the rehearsal of the orchestra that day. "My father was so nervous this morning. I guess some of it has rubbed off on me."

A slow smile spread across Mrs. Rose's face. "Ah, now I understand. But do you think you could just try to focus until the end of our lessons?"

Anna nodded and sighed. "I'll try."

When Mrs. Rose finally dismissed the class, Anna was the first one out the door and across the field to the rehearsal hall. She wished Eric were there with her, but her friend had been absent from school for the last couple of days.

She had stopped by his apartment the previous day to find out what was wrong. Eric's mother greeted her at the door, looking haggard. When Eric came out to talk to Anna, he looked equally tense.

"I brought this homework for you," Anna said, holding some papers out to Eric. "Mrs. Rose thought you should have this so you won't get too far behind."

Eric took the papers. "Thanks."

He was just about to close the door when Anna stopped him. "Aren't you going to tell me what's wrong?"

Eric hesitated. "I haven't been feeling that well. A really bad headache."

Was a headache, even a bad one, a reason to miss a couple of days of school? Anna didn't think so. "Is everything else okay?"

When Eric finally glanced up, his eyes were bleary looking, as if he hadn't been sleeping. Anna knew that look. She had seen it in Renata's eyes before her announcement that they were leaving Poland. But

Eric wasn't saying anything else, even when Anna asked him a second time. They said their good-byes and he closed the door.

Pushing those thoughts aside, she entered the rehearsal space and quickly found her spot to the left of the stage. She caught Papa's eye and waved. He raised his eyebrows to let her know he'd seen her. She was anxious for her father and for all the musicians. She knew they wanted nothing more than to impress the great Toscanini.

Mr. Huberman was already onstage and about to address the orchestra. "Ladies and gentlemen, we are indeed honored to be in the presence of a genius. He is not only a great musician, but a great friend to all of us who have escaped from persecution. Without further ado, I present to you Maestro Arturo Toscanini."

The orchestra members were on their feet, applauding for the man who made his way up the stairs and onto the stage. Anna craned her neck and stared at the conductor. She wasn't sure what she had expected to see. The words *genius* and *greatness* had conjured up images of something that was larger than life and not quite human. But Maestro Toscanini looked about as average as they came. He was not a particularly tall man. He had a thin fringe of white hair that encircled the back of his head, with just a tuft on top. His mustache was gray and full. His eyebrows were bushy and knitted together. If she had passed him on the street, she would not have given him a second look.

He bowed to the musicians and shook hands with Mr. Huberman. Then he simply said the name of the composer of the piece the orchestra was rehearsing: "Brahms." With that he raised his baton and began the rehearsal.

For the first two sections of the symphony, Toscanini didn't say a word. He conducted, listened, and remained silent. Anna thought things were going exceptionally well. She relaxed into the music and closed her eyes to listen for the sections that she loved so much. She hummed along and nodded her head in time with the music.

But with the start of the third section, Toscanini became upset. Without warning, he began to pound his baton on the music stand, screaming, "No, no, no!"

The musicians stopped in the middle of a musical passage and stared at one another and at their conductor, who was continuing to shout and rage. It didn't help that he was yelling in his native language of Italian. No one could understand a word he was saying. Finally, Mr. Huberman climbed back on the stage and spoke with Toscanini, who was still ranting in Italian. When Mr. Huberman looked back at the orchestra, his face was grim. "He says it's horrible," he began.

"*Terribile!*" Toscanini screamed in Italian. Anna didn't need an interpreter to translate the word. From the way Toscanini was behaving, he must have thought the orchestra members sounded like the barnyard animals that Anna heard when her father's former students used to play. Where was the compassionate man that her father had referred to? She was glued to her seat, every nerve in her body on edge. She felt sick to her stomach, like the time the German soldier had entered the train to check their papers. But this time, all her anxiety was focused on her father and the members of the orchestra. When she glanced over at Papa, he appeared to have gone quite pale.

Toscanini was still shouting, and from where Anna was sitting, it looked as if fire daggers were shooting from his eyes. He appeared so wound up Anna thought he might explode. Mr. Huberman continued to translate. "He says you all sound as if you are playing a Russian march, not a beautiful Brahms symphony."

Toscanini shouted some more.

"Now he says that you are playing as if there is mud in your instruments. This is meant to be light, not heavy and thick."

What was he talking about? To Anna's ears, the orchestra sounded as light as air.

Suddenly, Toscanini began to prance around the stage, lifting himself up on his toes and dancing a silly jig of some kind. Anna had to smile in spite of herself. He looked quite ridiculous and even some of the musicians snickered and giggled.

"There," shouted Mr. Huberman. "That's how he wants you to play. As if you were up on your toes and dancing."

"*Si, si,*" said Toscanini. "*Danza!*"

With that, Mr. Huberman left the stage and the rehearsal continued. Toscanini continued to interrupt from time to time, shouting some instruction that no one seemed to understand and waving his baton in the air as if it were a sword. Anna felt on edge until the rehearsal finally ended. Mr. Huberman approached her as she sat waiting for her father to pack up his instrument.

"And how do you think we sounded today, Miss Hirsch?"

"Wonderful!" Anna gushed.

Mr. Huberman paused and then said, "If you were to think of something that we might improve, what would that be?"

Anna paused. Mr. Huberman was asking her to critique the orchestra. Was that really okay? "I-I think the violins still need a bit more emotion when they play," she stammered. "Especially in the second section. It's meant to be a lullaby." Then she stopped and looked away.

Mr. Huberman raised his eyebrows and leaned forward. "I'm impressed with your observations, Miss Hirsch," he said. "And you are correct about the violins. You really are a budding musician."

Anna blushed a deep red. Then she frowned. "But I don't think Maestro Toscanini likes the orchestra very much."

"Oh, and what makes you think that?"

Anna couldn't believe Mr. Huberman was asking the question. Hadn't he heard all the yelling? "He was saying such terrible things about the music."

"And you think that because he was shouting he didn't like us?"

What else could she think? It was so obvious. She nodded.

"But you are quite wrong about that, Miss Hirsch. The only reason he was shouting is because he respects the orchestra so much he is willing to let the musicians know how he really feels."

Anna frowned. Respect? He had a funny way of showing it.

"If he didn't care, he would not have said a

word. Believe me, Miss Hirsch, the maestro is quite impressed with this orchestra."

)(

Papa didn't say much on the walk home with Anna. He looked completely downhearted. Anna didn't push him, not even to tell him what Mr. Huberman had said about how much Toscanini respected the musicians. She still wasn't sure that was true. When they reached the apartment, Papa disappeared inside, muttering something about needing to practice. Anna spotted Eric sitting on the stoop of his apartment building, and she walked over to say hello.

"You should have been there for the rehearsal, Eric. It was like nothing I've ever seen." She went on to tell him about Toscanini and even demonstrated the silly dance he had done. Finally, she collapsed in giggles and plopped down next to Eric. "Are you feeling any better?"

Eric didn't respond. It was only then that Anna noticed how distracted he appeared. He was staring off into space and barely smiling, not even at her description of the rehearsal or the dance. And the skin around his eyes was rubbed raw, as if he had been crying. "Eric, what's wrong?" He just shrugged his shoulders in reply and looked away again. "Please

tell me. You're my friend and I'm worried about you."
Anna pushed him.

Finally, Eric looked back at her. "My mother still
isn't happy about being here—in Palestine, I mean.
She finds it so hard. And she's having so much trouble
learning this new language."

Anna nodded. "We're all having trouble with that!
You should hear my grandmother. She can barely put
two Hebrew words together."

"I know," Eric agreed. "But I think it's more than
that. She's just so sad all the time. I think she just
really misses Poland," he added.

At that, Anna paused. She hadn't thought much
about Poland in the last few weeks, not since the day
she had discovered her clarinet was missing. In the
intervening time, the country of her birth had almost
vanished from her mind. Were there things that she
missed about her former home? Yes, she still missed
her friends, her lovely house, and the familiar sound
of her language being spoken on the streets. But she
didn't miss the angry people who were targeting
Jewish citizens. She didn't miss the sight of signs on
stores warning that Jews were not welcome. She didn't
miss the thugs who threatened old men, even when
they were minding their own business and not both-
ering anyone. She had seen with her own eyes how

conditions in Poland were getting worse and worse, and Papa had told her that Jewish citizens in other countries were also suffering. She didn't miss any of that.

Since their arrival in Palestine, Anna had only received one letter from Stefan, even though she had written him several times. In it, Stefan had written that all the Jewish families in Krakow were more afraid than ever. He was still trying to talk his father into finding a way to get out, but so far, they were stuck. That letter had arrived a month ago. Since then, there had been nothing from Stefan—as if he had disappeared.

"My father says we should be grateful that Mr. Huberman was able to get us out of there," Anna reminded Eric. "I know it's hard to get used to living in a new place, but I think it's even worse back in Poland."

"You're right," Eric replied. "I just wish that my mother saw it the way your father does." Then he exhaled, as if wanting to push away the thoughts. "You know what? I've been promising to take you exploring ever since we arrived here. How about tomorrow, after school?"

What Anna really wanted was to hear the orchestra rehearse on its second day with Toscanini. But Eric's eyes had suddenly brightened when he talked about going on an adventure. A moment ago, he had looked so discouraged. There would be more rehearsals to come, she reasoned. This sounded like it could be fun.

"Sure," she replied. "Let's do it."

CHAPTER 29

Eric and Anna headed out the door of the schoolroom as soon as Mrs. Rose dismissed them.

"Where are we going?" Anna asked, following Eric down the hill toward the main road.

"We're going to the beach."

At that, she stopped short. *The beach!* She had wanted to go there ever since she spied the sea from their apartment balcony on the first day. And she certainly wanted an adventure. But maybe this was too much. Baba knew that Anna was going to be with Eric for the afternoon. She had even given her some money to buy a snack. But she assumed they would stay close to the apartment building. Neither she, nor Anna's father, would have approved of a trip to the beach—at least not without adult supervision. Just a week earlier, Anna had learned that there had been an attack on a convoy of trucks in the northern part of Palestine. The Jewish driver and several others had been killed. Jewish groups had retaliated with an attack on Arab workers and also killed several people. The British military had imposed a mandatory curfew. Everyone had to be in their homes by dusk. Perhaps this was not a good time to be out wandering on the streets.

"Wait, Eric." He was already steps ahead and turned at the sound of her voice. "I'm not sure we should do this."

"You said you wanted some fun."

"I know," she replied. "But I don't think my father would want us to go to the beach alone."

Eric retraced his steps to stand next to Anna. "I know what I'm doing. We'll walk down to the beach, put our feet in the sea, and then come back home. Nothing bad is going to happen."

It was an appealing offer. And the urge to go with Eric was beginning to take hold. She remembered that when her family had vacationed at the Baltic Sea, the water was so cold that when she dipped her foot in, her leg had cramped all the way up. Papa had told her that the sea in Tel Aviv was much warmer, even though the weather had turned cool. Anna was wearing a jacket and a knitted cap pulled down on her forehead.

"Do you even know how to get there?" she asked weakly.

Eric grinned. "Just follow me." And with that, he began walking again. Anna hesitated for a second and then took off after him as he began to wind his way down streets, some so narrow that only pedestrians could pass. She felt turned around in circles and struggled to keep up with her friend. The last thing she wanted was to lose him in the crowd and be left on her own.

"I know what direction the sea is in," Eric called over his shoulder, as if he knew she doubted him. "I can smell it! We'll just keep heading that way."

Anna followed. Eric had always proved he was a wizard at finding his way around, and she hoped that he would do the same now. Every now and then, armored tanks with British soldiers on board rolled by on the streets of Tel Aviv. Anna shuddered at the sight but had no time to think too much about what it meant. Eric was still plowing ahead and Anna tried to stay close to his heels. Despite the cool weather, she could feel her face start to grow hot and the sweat begin to gather across her neck and back. And just as she was about to shout out to Eric to stop, they rounded a curve and there it was.

The Mediterranean Sea lay ahead of them, stretching out to an infinite horizon. The water shimmered

and glistened in the sunlight, reflecting a kaleido-
scope of colors from blue to green, with yellow and red
tints thrown into the mix. There was a seawall made
of giant rocks in the distance that calmed the water
closer to shore. Gentle waves lapped up on the beach
and rippled across the sand that spread for miles in
both directions.

Anna and Eric ran down a small hill and over to
the water's edge. Anna threw off her jacket, kicked
off her shoes, and waded in. The water tickled as it
licked at her toes. Yes, the temperature was definitely
warmer than the Baltic Sea and surprisingly warm for
this November day, just as Papa had said it would be.
She hiked her trousers up and waded farther in, right
up to her knees. Then she scooped some water in her
hands and threw it high in the air, shrieking and covering her head as the spray came down on top of her.
She could taste the salt in her mouth. Eric was right
by her side, running across the shallow waves and
kicking his heels up into the air. Anna threw back her
head, spread her arms wide, and laughed out loud.
She wondered why she had been so nervous to come
here with Eric. There was nothing to be afraid of.

The beach was relatively quiet, though here and
there, young children were building sand castles
while their parents looked on. Only a few people were

brave enough to swim. While the water was reasonably warm and the sun shone down on them, the air was cool and a biting wind was blowing across the beach, lifting a fine layer of sand up into the air. When Anna turned her back, she felt the sharp pricks of sand against her skin.

After a while, she and Eric stopped wading in the sea and Anna bought some dates and nuts from a vendor on the beach using the money Baba had given her. Then she went in search of some flowers. She had not yet added to her dried flower collection. And the wild flowers that grew by the far edge of the sand would be perfect. She picked a couple of flowers that were as blue as the seawater, and one that was bright red. She would figure out what they were later. For now, she carefully placed them in her pocket so they wouldn't be crushed.

Finally, she sank down onto the sand next to Eric. "I'm glad you convinced me to come," she said, offering him some dates.

Eric grinned. His bright red hair was standing straight up in the breeze and he was trying unsuccessfully to smooth it down. "Me too. This is the most fun I've had in a long time."

Anna nodded and stared back out at the sea. "Do you ever think about what you want to be when you're older?" she asked. She lifted up a handful of sand and let it run through her fingers, holding it away from the wind.

Eric shrugged. "I'm not sure. I think about being a teacher. Or maybe I'll be a travel guide. I do like to go exploring." He flashed a grin. "What about you? Do you know what you want to do?"

"Oh, yes," she replied. "I want to be a musician like my father." After listening to the orchestra rehearsing for the opening concert, she had become more and more certain of that. Over the last couple of months, she had continued with her clarinet lessons under her father's watchful eye. It wasn't always pretty. She knew that sometimes she still sounded a bit like a crow when she played. But she was getting better and better; she was sure of that. She still dreamed that one day, somehow, she would have her own clarinet and not have to borrow Papa's.

The sun was beginning to slip down toward the horizon. Families were packing up their chairs and blankets and climbing back up the small hill behind them to their homes. It was time for Anna and Eric to head home as well. It had been a perfect after-noon, and Anna couldn't wait to tell Papa and Baba all about it. Next time she would bring her swim-suit for sure. Eric stood up and extended his hand to help Anna. She pulled herself up and gave him one more playful shove before running back to the water's edge to retrieve her shoes and jacket. Eric was right behind her. But just as they reached the shoreline, she heard a deep, booming blast that echoed across the beach from some distance away. Anna jumped as the sand under her feet suddenly shifted. She stared off to where the blast had come from and was alarmed to see black smoke billowing and pouring across the sky.

CHAPTER
30

"What is that?" Anna asked. Her heart felt as if it had suddenly clenched into a tight fist. The smoke in the distance was growing thicker and blacker, and the remaining families on the beach were running in all directions, dragging their little ones behind them.

"We need to get out of here." Eric's voice was loud and urgent. He grabbed Anna's jacket and shoes, shoving them into her hands, and then grabbed his own. The two of them raced up the hill and onto the street, which had become flooded with people running with their heads down. As they struggled to put their shoes back on, they were followed by armored vehicles moving in formation. Announcements were being blasted over a loudspeaker. But the broadcast was in Hebrew, and despite her growing skill in the language, Anna could not catch what was being said.

"Can you tell me what's happening, please?" She stopped a woman who was scurrying past, carrying parcels under one arm and protecting her head with the other.

"Take cover," the woman shouted as she passed. "There could be a second attack!" And then she was gone.

Attack? Who is attacking? She looked at Eric, eyes frantically searching his face. He had grown pale and his eyes behind his glasses bulged with fear. "Eric, which way do we go?"

At first he looked confused. He glanced to the right, then behind them, and then right again. "Eric!" she repeated, louder this time.

Finally, he shook his head and pointed up a road. "This way. Follow me," he shouted.

Anna sprinted after him. At one point, she nearly plowed headlong into a British army man who marched past with his rifle at the ready. He shouted at her. "Didn't you hear the warning? Get off the street."

Eric grabbed her arm and they darted around the soldier and ran some more, turning to the left and then to the right, passing under an archway and across a park. Anna didn't remember having come this way to get to the beach, but she followed Eric, hoping and praying that he knew where he was going. The sun had nearly disappeared behind the hills in the distance and the sky was losing its light. *Papa will be frantic with worry*, Anna thought as she continued to follow Eric through the streets, which were becoming more and more deserted. The sudden quiet was almost more terrifying than the commotion of moments earlier. And still they ran, until finally, Eric slowed and came to a stop. Anna came up next to him, breathing heavily. He looked up the street and then down, and then up once more.

"Eric, where are we?" Anna was struggling to catch her breath.

"I … I'm not sure. I thought I knew the way. But I'm just not sure."

"But you said you knew where we were going!" Eric knew how to get everywhere. He had a sense of direction that was unequaled. But this time, he held his hands up as if he were surrendering.

"I think I'm lost."

Lost? No, that wasn't possible. Soon the mandatory curfew would take effect. And then what? Would they be arrested? Would they be shot? Anna squeezed her eyes shut and tried to block the wild thoughts that were galloping through her brain.

The whole outing suddenly felt as if it had been one big mistake. Gone was the pleasure of having discovered the beach and tasted the spray of saltwater, of collecting flowers and playing in the sand. She was angry that she had followed Eric and not listened to her gut, which had told her not to go. And then she stopped herself. Eric already looked so tormented. It wasn't fair of her to put all of this on him. She reached out and touched his arm. "Okay," she said. "Let's just try and figure out what we're going to do."

Just then, as they stood under a street lamp, shivering in the cool evening air, a car pulled up and stopped next to them. Its headlights beamed a spooky glow that lit up the road in front. The driver rolled down his window and nodded toward Anna and Eric.

Anna squinted to make out the man who leaned out from behind the wheel. He was younger than Papa, with a face that was long and narrow. He had dark eyes, a short beard, and eyebrows that were so bushy it looked as if two caterpillars had walked across his forehead and nested there. An embroidered linen scarf was draped over his head, held in place by a black braided cord. He scratched at his beard with one hand while the other rested on the steering wheel. Alarm bells were going off in Anna's mind. This was an Arab man. Anna had seen others like him in the

market. She hadn't been frightened then. But everything felt different here on these darkened streets.
Frantically, she searched left and right, hoping to see
someone else there. The streets were empty.

The man was talking, saying something in Arabic.
Then he reached a spindly arm out the window,
pulled open the back door, and waited. The car was
rattling and belching smoke from its rear exhaust. It
looked as unsafe as the man who was driving it.

"What does he want?" Eric whispered.

"I think he's offering us a ride."

The man nodded toward the back seat and spoke
again. And then he smiled, a broad grin that reached
from ear to ear. *This is so wrong,* Anna's mind
screamed. *And dangerous!* Who was this man? How
did they know he was safe? If Papa or Baba knew
that they were taking a ride from this stranger, they
would have gone crazy. "What should we do?" she
whispered.

"I don't think we have much of a choice," Eric
replied with as much uncertainty as Anna was
feeling. "We don't have any other way to get home.
But stay close to me," he added. "If he tries anything,
we'll jump out the back."

Anna shuddered and shifted from one foot to
the other. She had already ignored her instincts in
following Eric to the beach. Was she going to ignore

them a second time? But there really was no choice here. To wander the streets in the dark would put them in even greater danger. She nodded at Eric. *Agreed!* They approached the car, got in, and closed the door.

The stranger eyed them through the rearview mirror. "Asim," he said, tapping his chest.

"That must be his name," Eric muttered before the man continued talking, a string of rapid Arabic words that meant nothing to Anna.

"I think he wants to know where to take us," she said. What was he even doing out driving at this time? Normally, Arabic drivers needed an army escort to be in this part of Tel Aviv. Perhaps in the commotion following the explosion, he had simply been forgotten. *The explosion!* She still had no idea what had happened.

Anna and Eric remained silent. Eric was pressed against the back door and Anna was as close to him as she could get without sitting on his lap. Asim was staring at them, waiting for a response. Then he spoke again, pantomiming his hands turning the steering wheel and then shrugging his shoulders as if he were asking for instructions on where to drive.

Eric leaned forward and spoke in slow Hebrew. "The apartment buildings close to the Levant Fairgrounds. That's where we live."

Asim continued to stare at them, knitting his bushy eyebrows together.

"Let me try," Anna said. She took a deep breath and repeated, "Levant. Levant." She said it louder the second time, as if raising her voice would help her make herself understood. And all the while, she kept thinking of Papa. He would be scared to death if she didn't get home soon.

Suddenly, Asim broke into another wide grin and nodded energetically. "Levant," he replied. Then he turned around, put the car into gear, and took off.

Eric and Anna remained silently pressed together in the back seat. Anna stared out the window, desperate to catch sight of some landmark that was familiar. So far, nothing was recognizable. There was a photograph on the dashboard of Asim's car. Anna could make out two young children, seated next to each other, faces solemn and eyes as big as saucers. When Asim caught her stare in his rearview mirror, he nodded toward the picture and then touched his chest.

"*Ab*," he said.

Anna recognized the word, which was so close to its Hebrew equivalent. "I think he's their father," she whispered to Eric. She nodded toward the photo. "Those must be his kids."

Asim nodded. "Sada," he said, pointing to the little girl. "Ali," he added, indicating the boy.

Anna smiled. Her body was still tightly wound, and her stomach was still in knots. But it was somehow reassuring to discover that this stranger was a father. It made him seem less dangerous. He continued to drive, turning this way and that. Finally, Anna spotted their apartment complex up ahead. Relief washed over her. "There it is," she cried, pointing up ahead.

Asim nodded. "Levant," he replied.

A second later, all of Anna's relief disappeared as she spotted her father standing outside, pacing anxiously. Eric's mother and father were there too. But instead of pulling into the driveway next to their building, Asim suddenly stopped the car some distance away. He turned and stared at Anna and Eric. Then he pointed to their door and muttered something.

"I don't think he wants to go all the way up there," Eric said.

Anna nodded. It was probably best not to have their families meet this man. As grateful as Papa would be for their return, in this time of heightened tension in the country, he would still be distraught to know they had accepted a ride from an Arabic man.

She and Eric climbed out of the car and stood next to it while Asim rolled down his window. In the dusky light of the street lamp, it looked as if his eyebrows were dancing across his forehead. He smiled once more, touched his temple, and said, "*Salaam.*"

Once again, Anna recognized the Arabic word. He was saying good-bye to them. "*Shalom,*" she replied in Hebrew. Then he drove off, his exhaust belching and blowing smoke.

Eric and Anna turned and sprinted up the driveway. Anna was immediately scooped up by Papa, who squeezed her so hard, she nearly lost her breath.

"Annichka! Oh, my darling girl. I was sick with worry. What happened? Where were you?"

Papa hugged and squeezed and wouldn't let her go. Finally, she managed to pull away. "I'm so sorry, Papa," she cried. "We went to the beach." When she saw his stricken face, she added, "I know, I know! We thought we knew where we were. But after the explosion …"

"Yes, we were even more frantic when we heard the blast. A train was derailed with a grenade in Lod, about ten miles from here. We were just going to begin searching for you—Eric's parents and me. We didn't know where to start. You're not hurt, are you?" He examined her face, searching for an injury or cut, or something.

Eric was in an animated conversation with his father. His mother looked as if she might pass out. Her face was stamped with terror. Anna raised her voice to make sure that Eric's parents could hear her.

"No, we're fine." Eric's father stopped talking and looked in her direction. "Eric was trying to find the way back here. But it was getting dark and we weren't sure what to do."

"How did you ever get home?" Papa asked.

Anna and Eric exchanged glances across the driveway as an unspoken agreement passed between them. "Eric finally figured it out," Anna said. "It just took longer than we thought."

Papa squeezed Anna once more. Before going inside, Anna hung back with Eric.

"Please don't be long, Annichka," Papa said. "Your grandmother was so sick with worry, she had to lie down. She will want to see for herself that you are okay."

Anna promised she would be up in a few minutes.

"I'm so sorry I got us lost," Eric moaned when their parents had left. "I made such a mess of things."

"It's not your fault," Anna replied. "We would have been fine if that explosion hadn't happened."

"I just got so mixed up; I didn't know which way to go."

"I know. Please stop feeling so bad about this. We're both fine. Nothing happened. We were lucky that man came along." Anna pointed toward Eric's apartment. "Will you be in trouble?"

Eric hung his head. "Maybe. My parents were pretty upset. It's not going to make my mother any happier about being here, that's for sure."

"Come with me tomorrow to the rehearsal," Anna pleaded. "It will make you feel better." She knew it didn't sound like much of an offer. But Eric was looking so miserable and she was desperate to find a way to help lift his mood.

"Okay," he said, nodding yes.

CHAPTER
31

While Anna and Eric were still allowed to attend orchestra rehearsals after their schoolwork was done, traveling around the city without adult supervision was off limits—at least for now. Anna didn't mind. She had had enough of exploring for a while. She was content to go to classes and then head for the rehearsal hall. Eric often came with her, though it seemed to Anna as if the light had gone out of him. He had been so bold and so curious before their unfortunate outing. Now he was quiet and withdrawn. Some days he just went home after classes without even saying good-bye to her. *I'm just going to give him some time*, she told herself. She figured he still felt bad about getting them lost. In the meantime, the rehearsals for the first concert were steaming ahead.

In addition to practicing the Brahms symphony, the musicians had gone on to learn the other four pieces for the challenging program that was being prepared for opening night. There were still days when Toscanini appeared to be jumping out of his skin as he ranted at the musicians to speed up, slow down, play softer, play louder, feel the music. When he yelled, it was only in Italian, but somehow the musicians understood. Even Anna, from her position in the audience, began to understand what he was trying to communicate.

The weeks were speeding by and it was only days away from the opening concert. Miraculously, the concert hall was nearing completion. As promised, the workers were nowhere to be seen during the day-time rehearsals. They came out only at night, like bats, to hammer and saw and paint and plaster. The next day, it was as if tiny elves had worked through the night to get the hall one step closer to completion. Gone was the tin roof, the floor was now a proper shining wooden floor, and the seats were being lined up to accommodate the crowd that would be there on opening night.

These days, Mr. Huberman was too busy to stop and talk to Anna. She waved shyly to him from time to time, and he always returned the greeting before he scurried across the concert hall, carrying sheet music, talking with Toscanini, approving the program that was being printed, or doing whatever else needed to be done. Everyone seemed to be demanding something of him, and he patiently stopped to address all their questions and problems.

One afternoon, Anna was walking home from one of the last rehearsals, her head still filled with the musical notes that had echoed through the hall. She couldn't wait to tell Eric how Toscanini had gone up on his tiptoes to demonstrate how lightly he had wanted the musicians to play a particular passage. She hadn't seen her friend for a few days and she wanted to have a good long talk with him. As she approached the apartment complex, she could see him emerging from his building and she sped up to catch him. But suddenly, she stopped in her tracks. Eric was dragging a big suitcase behind him. Was he going on a trip? How was that possible so close to the opening night of the symphony? She began to run toward the building, calling out his name as she got closer. He stopped, put down the case, and waited for her to catch up.

"Why have you got that suitcase?" she asked, breathless. "Are you going somewhere?"

Eric looked down before replying. "We're leaving. Going back to Poland." He nodded toward the road, where his parents were piling suitcases onto the roof of a car. His younger sister stood close by, holding a doll in her arms and watching the whole thing.

What is he talking about? She had a sudden, fleeting memory of another conversation with Renata that had started just like this. "You're what? You mean now?"

"Yes. We're taking this car back to Haifa and then sailing away this evening."

Anna couldn't believe what she was hearing. "But why?" she asked.

"It's just become impossible for my family to be here any longer, especially my mother," he said. "I told you all of this."

Yes, he had told her that his mother found it hard to adjust to life in Palestine, but they all did. That didn't mean they should leave.

"And then after that explosion happened and my parents thought they might have lost me ..." Eric's voice trailed off.

Anna was fumbling about, trying to find something to say. "We were all really scared about that. But nothing happened to us." She stared at him a moment longer. "I can't believe you're leaving."

Eric shrugged. "They've been talking about it for a while. But it all came together a couple of days ago. My mother refuses to stay another day. And there's nothing my father can do to convince her."

"Eric, please stay!" she begged. "Maybe you can

move in with us. I'm sure I can convince Papa." She knew she was sounding desperate.

Eric shook his head. "My parents would never agree. We have to stay together as a family. There's no other option."

"Aren't you ... aren't you afraid of going back?" Anna asked this carefully and hesitantly.

At that, he looked away. "I'm sure it will be fine."

Fine? Fine! She wanted to scream out at Eric that nothing in Poland was fine. Had he not heard the radio reports? Every day the conditions for Jewish people across Europe were getting worse and worse. Hitler was gaining power. The laws and rules that he had introduced in Germany to restrict the freedom of Jewish people were sweeping across Europe into Hungary, Czechoslovakia, and, yes, Poland. Every day there were new rants by Hitler. "The symbol of evil is the living shape of the Jews," he screamed one day through the radio. "We shall regain our health by eliminating the Jews," he blasted in another message. Each time, Papa or Baba quickly turned the radio off when Anna entered the room, but not before she had heard his hateful attack. Jewish families were clamoring to get out of Europe, but there were fewer and fewer places for them to go. Didn't Eric know that? Didn't his family know that? How could they go back to a place that offered no security? It may be difficult in Palestine, but at least they were free here. She wanted to say all of that to Eric, but to what end? Would that stop him from leaving? She knew the answer to that was no.

"Do you know what your father is going to do when you get back?" she asked, quieter still. She knew that since they had left, Jewish musicians were being barred from playing in the orchestras of Europe.

Eric shook his head. "We have relatives who are still there. They're going to help us get settled."

There was a long pause. "You're going to miss the concert." Anna said this in barely a whisper.

"I know."

Eric looked as if he might break down, and Anna felt close to tears herself. She was terrified for Eric's safety back in Poland. And she was losing a friend here in Palestine. This was not what she had imagined.

Eric's father was calling him. The car was ready to leave. There was no more time to talk. Anna stared at Eric another moment and then flew forward and threw her arms around his neck. "Stay safe," she cried.

"I'll try to write," he said. He bent to pick up his suitcase, and stepped away to join his family. The car revved its engine and pulled away, leaving a cloud of dust behind. And a moment later, Eric was gone.

CHAPTER

32

Anna disappeared into her bedroom, refusing to speak to Papa or even Baba when she tried to offer Anna a slice of her apple cake. She threw herself down on the bed and buried her face in her pillow, squeezing her eyes shut and trying to stop the tears that were dampening the sheets under her face. *Why is everything always so hard? So complicated?* She had just started to feel like this country might provide a comfortable home for her and her family. She didn't feel singled out here. She was learning the language, understanding the people. She was beginning to feel like a *sabra*. And now it felt as if everything had shattered around her. The city felt less safe, and her only good friend was leaving. It wasn't fair. And yes, she knew she was feeling sorry for herself and she should be worrying more about Eric. But in that moment, a mountain of frustration came crashing down on her. She felt hopeless and terribly sad.

Finally, she rolled over on her side and glanced at the bedroom wall. One of the new flowers that she had collected from the beach and dried was mounted in a tiny frame that her father had found for her. After looking it up in a book on flowers, she had discovered that it was a wild poppy, so much like the two red poppies that she had found in Poland—one given to Renata and the other placed on her mother's headstone before they left. This new flower reminded her of the adventure to the beach she had shared with Eric. She would never forget that—or him.

There was another soft knock and Baba's worried face appeared in the doorway. "May I come in?" Anna nodded and sat up, wiping her face. Baba sat down on the bed next to her. "I know about Eric," she said. "I'm so sorry."

Anna nodded again, knowing how hard it must be for Baba to talk to her about this painful moment. "What will happen to him, Baba? I mean, when he and his family are back in Poland."

Baba sighed. "I wish I could tell you that everything will be okay. But I'm afraid I can't."

"I don't know what makes me sadder," Anna said,

"to think about Eric leaving here or to imagine him back there."

For a moment neither one of them spoke. Then Baba said, "You know, Eric's family is not the only one to go. Your father told me that two violinists from the orchestra along with their families are also going back, one to Germany and the other to Poland. Apparently, they are also finding it too difficult here."

Anna hadn't known that. "But what's going to happen to the orchestra if Eric's father and others leave?"

"Your father said that Mr. Huberman is replacing them with local musicians. The concert will go on as planned."

Anna was silent again. "It's been hard for me, too, being here in Palestine," she finally said. She told Baba about the times when she couldn't understand what Mrs. Rose or anyone else was saying. She talked about the mosquitoes that were so bad after a rainfall that not only did she have to keep her arms and legs covered, she also had to keep her mouth closed for fear that she might swallow a few of them. She talked about missing Stefan and Renata and their house in Krakow. And then she hesitated and continued more softly. "And then a grenade drops on a train and I worry that something worse might happen."

"Yes," nodded Baba. "And on those days, I always remind myself what a miracle it was that Mr. Huberman was able to get us out of Poland." There was another long pause before Baba continued talking. "Did you know that there are more than a thousand people he brought here? Not just the seventy musicians, but their family members, like me and so many others."

Was it really that many people whose lives had been saved? It didn't make Eric's leaving any easier, but yes, Anna knew there was much she had to be grateful for.

"Come, Annichka," Baba said at last. "I offered you cake before and you turned me down. Won't you have a small piece?"

At that, Anna had to smile. Food was her grandmother's favorite remedy. And while it would not take the pain away, it would remind her how lucky she was to live in this loving family. She nodded at Baba.

"And then, I would love to listen to you practice the clarinet. And it would please your father so much. He is terribly worried about you." She paused and then said, "You and your father can take turns on his clarinet. The music will help us all."

Anna wasn't sure she was ready to leave the security of her room just yet. But Baba's request was tempting. Playing the clarinet and losing herself in some music would help take her mind off Eric—at least for a little while.

Anna wiped her face once more and finally smiled again at her grandmother. "Perhaps Papa can also teach me some of what Maestro Toscanini is teaching him—minus the shouting in Italian!"

Anna's grandmother hugged her tightly. "Wonderful!"

CHAPTER 33

The night of the concert had finally arrived, and even though Papa kept insisting that they needed just a few more days, "to make it perfect," Anna knew it was perfect already. She also knew she would never convince her father of that. She dressed for the concert, putting on her best dress—the same one she had worn on the day she accompanied Papa to Warsaw for his audition in front of Mr. Huberman. And just like before, she wrapped the green scarf from Renata around her neck. Even though this time she didn't need it for luck, it was Anna's way of bringing her best friend with her to the concert. This was also the same outfit she had been wearing when she met Eric. She was trying not to think about him too much; it only plunged her into sadness. Even though it had only been a few days since Eric's departure, Anna hoped that a letter would arrive from him soon. It was hard to wait.

Papa was running around the apartment, looking just as lost and nervous as he had looked on the first day Maestro Toscanini had arrived to lead the rehearsal. He was wearing a formal black tailcoat, a white vest, and a white shirt, which Baba had starched so crisply it looked as if it might stand up on its own. He tugged at the collar and readjusted his waistband until Anna finally had to pull his hands away. "You look very handsome, Papa," she said. He smiled weakly in return.

Tonight, even Baba looked anxious. She fussed in the mirror with her hair and adjusted her dress a dozen times. "Annichka," she moaned. "I look old and ... ugly!"

Anna laughed. "Baba, you look beautiful." And she believed it was true. She couldn't remember when she had seen her grandmother so dressed up. She wore a long black dress with a blue silk shawl wrapped around her shoulders, and her special pearl necklace around her neck. "You look like a schoolgirl." Baba blushed and grabbed her granddaughter, holding her in a tight hug. Then, for good measure, she spit three times onto her fingers. Anna laughed. Those superstitions would never leave her grandmother.

They walked over to the concert hall together, joining the huge crowd of people who had been lucky enough to get tickets. Close to the site, Papa turned to say good-bye to Anna and Baba. He would enter from a back door and join the musicians onstage. He bent to give her a hug. "Tonight, I will be playing just for you, Annichka," he whispered in her ear. She wanted to wish him luck but didn't trust herself to speak. So she just returned the hug and then watched him walk away.

The fairground was packed with people. In addition to the two thousand entering the hall with tickets, there were tens of thousands of people setting up beach chairs and blankets in the area. The concert was going to be broadcast through speakers that were mounted on lampposts. Anna knew that some of these people had been here all day, holding onto the perfect spot where they could hear the concert being played and feel as if they were a part of it all.

She and Baba walked into the hall and found their seats. The excitement was rising inside of Anna and threatening to overflow. She was practically shaking with anticipation. The orchestra members were warming up onstage. The violinists and cellists were tightening their bows, and the wind and brass players were blowing into their clarinets, trumpets, and oboes. Anna caught her father's eye. He smiled broadly and then went back to tuning up.

Anna turned in her seat to look around at the crowd. Behind her she recognized some of the construction workers who were responsible for building the concert hall. As promised, Mr. Huberman had supplied them with tickets to this first concert. They looked uncomfortable in their stiff collars and tight dress jackets.

The crowd was starting to settle. The orchestra members rested their instruments. The lights dimmed. A spotlight shone on the stage as Mr. Huberman entered and walked to a spot at the center. "Today is a day of victory," he began. "This orchestra, our orchestra, is comprised of men and women who have been fortunate to escape the hatred that is sweeping across Europe. We pray for our brothers and our sisters who are still there and struggling to survive."

Eric, Anna thought again. *And Stefan. Please let them both stay safe.*

"Let us raise our instruments and our voices against that hatred and show the world that we are strong and will not be stopped. Ladies and gentlemen, I present to you the Palestine Symphony Orchestra."

The crowd was on its feet cheering and applauding even before Maestro Toscanini had taken his place behind the music stand. He had to wait minutes with his arms raised before the crowd settled once more. And then the concert began.

Anna sat on the edge of her seat, listening as the musicians attacked each piece with more energy and passion than she had ever heard. The music soared, then became quiet, then soared again. The orchestra played like poetry and fireworks mixed together. Maestro Toscanini held the musicians together like the captain of a ship. It was as if his baton was talking to them, setting the tempo, unifying the performers and still allowing each section of the orchestra to have its moment to shine. She gave herself over to the music entirely, allowing it to wash over and through her, savoring every note, feeling every change in speed and mood. The music nudged memories out of her that tugged at her heart: Renata, Stefan, even Sabina who had played like sunshine, Baba's cooking, the puppet show her mother had taken her to as a child, picking flowers, the gentle waves on the Tel Aviv beach, Eric. She thought about all of that and more.

Every piece was followed by a standing ovation that seemed to go on forever. At one point, Anna could even hear the crowd outside cheering with appreciation.

And then, it was over. The last note had been played, the last bow taken. The crowd was beginning to leave the hall. Some of the construction workers whom Anna had seen in the audience were helping tidy up and straighten the music stands onstage. She thought they looked so much more comfortable now that they had removed their jackets and rolled up their sleeves. Anna was still in her seat, breathless and exhausted. She felt as if every muscle in her body had been humming along with every note of every piece that the orchestra had played.

"Stay here, Annichka," said Baba. "I'm going to find your father. Tonight we will celebrate with my most delicious pancakes stuffed with apples." Baba dabbed at her eyes. "It was beautiful, puh, puh, puh," she said, her voice shaking. "Simply beautiful."

Anna sank down into her seat, resting her head on the back of the chair and closing her eyes.

"I hope this doesn't mean that the concert put you to sleep."

Anna opened her eyes, sat up in her seat, and turned to face Mr. Huberman, who was standing next to her. She grinned. "I was trying to see if I could remember every note that you played."

"And were you successful?"

"I think I might have been. I know I won't ever forget this."

Mr. Huberman took a long, deep breath and looked around the concert hall. "I don't think I will either," he said. His eyes came back to rest on Anna. "Did you approve of the performance, Miss Hirsch?"

Anna nodded, eyes shining. "The violins were especially emotional during the lullaby," she added.

Mr. Huberman looked thoughtful. "I have some things that I still must do this evening. But I'd like you to come and see me—perhaps tomorrow. I have something for you."

Before Anna could ask what it was, Mr. Huberman turned and walked away.

CHAPTER

34

The next day, Anna made her way across the fair-ground to the concert hall to see Mr. Huberman. She had not had much sleep the night before. She had stayed up with Papa and Baba for hours, talking about the concert, reliving the highlights, analyzing every note that had been played.

"Did you see how pleased Toscanini looked?" Papa said. "I've never seen him smile so much. He even told us afterward that it was the happiest moment of his life!" Papa sighed. "I will never forget this."

Baba, true to her word, had stuffed them with pan-cakes and other sweet treats. Anna remained awake long after she went to bed, her mind still replaying the music.

In the morning, she was tired, but also curious about this meeting. Mr. Huberman said he had something for her and she wondered what that could possibly be. But she also had her own surprise for the maestro, something she had brought for him.

She opened the door to the concert hall and walked inside. It was quiet, and for a moment, Anna found it hard to believe that just hours earlier this place had hummed and throbbed with the sounds of the symphony. Every chair was back in place, every piece of paper removed from the floor, every stand on the stage waiting for the musicians to take their places and begin to play again. There would be no rehearsal today; it was a day off for everyone. But in a back corner, seated behind a small desk, Anna spied Mr. Huberman hunched over some papers, his glasses poised on the tip of his nose. He was wearing a suit and tie—as always, so properly and formally dressed.

Anna approached the desk and then stopped, uncertain of whether or not she should interrupt him. A moment later, he looked up and caught sight of her. He stood up, moved out from behind his desk, and came to stand in front of her. "Miss Hirsch," he said, smiling broadly. "Thank you so much for coming in to see me today."

"Did you stay all night?" Anna blurted out.

Mr. Huberman laughed softly. "No, I did manage

to go home and get a few hours of sleep. Not much, mind you. My mind was still buzzing with last night's performance."

"Mine too!" Anna exclaimed.

"The reviews of our opening have been wonderful," Mr. Huberman added. "I think our orchestra will be a great success in this country."

Now seemed the perfect moment for Anna to give him her present. "There is something that I brought you," she said. With that, she reached into the pocket of her jacket and pulled out the small flower, now dried and framed, that she had collected from the beach the day she had gone there with Eric. But as she went to hand it to him, she felt shy suddenly, and looked away. It was such a little gift, not at all worthy of this great man. *He's going to think I'm silly for giving him something so unimportant.*

Mr. Huberman stepped forward, taking the framed flower gently from her hands. "Is this something that you made?"

"Um, well, yes," she stammered. "It's a wild poppy." She went on to explain that she collected and dried flowers as a hobby. "I gave one almost like this to my best friend, and left another one in Poland … on my mother's grave … before we left." *Could I sound any more clumsy?* She felt as though she was making a mess of a situation that she had hoped would be simple.

"Did you know that I was born in Poland?"

She hadn't known that. "Do you miss it?"

He looked thoughtful. "I miss the Poland that once was."

She nodded and thought once more about Eric and Stefan.

"Thank you for this beautiful gift," Mr. Huberman said, bowing slightly. "I shall treasure it." He placed the flower carefully on his desk. "And now," he continued, "as I told you last night, I have a gift for you." He walked behind his desk, reached into a drawer, and pulled something out, which he quickly hid behind his back as he walked over to her.

"I think you need your own instrument, Miss Hirsch," he said. And then, from behind his back, he pulled out a shining new clarinet and placed it into Anna's hands.

She could not believe what he had given her. She held the clarinet in front of her as if it were a delicate piece of glass. "But, it's too much," she stammered.

Mr. Huberman waved the objection away. "Not at all. It will make me happy to know that you have your very own clarinet." He leaned forward and whispered. "Make sure you don't lose this one."

She looked up at Mr. Huberman, her eyes brimming with tears. "I promise I'll keep it safe," she began. "But I don't know how to thank you."

"Practice hard," he said. "That will make me very happy. Practice makes perfect, you know."

Anna smiled—Mr. Huberman sounded just like her father. She clutched the clarinet to her chest, scarcely able to believe that this was now hers. Yes, she would practice every day, and make her papa and Mr. Huberman proud, along with her mother and Baba, and Eric, too. No more barnyard animals. She would play like the rolling sand of the desert and like the waves on the sea.

"Perhaps you will be the next generation to play in my lovely orchestra," added Mr. Huberman. "Think about how wonderful that would be."

Anna smiled up at Mr. Huberman. "Yes, that would be wonderful." And then, with her beautiful new clarinet in her hands, she turned and headed home.

Author's Note

Although *The Sound of Freedom* is a work of fiction, it is based on a true story about a famous Jewish musician by the name of Bronislaw Huberman, who was born in 1890. Even as a child, he was thought to be a genius on the violin. At the age of eight, his father moved him from Poland, the country of his birth, to Germany, where he studied with some of the greatest violinists of that time. He played in concerts in the U.S., in Russia, and across Europe.

But by the early 1930s, Huberman was becoming quite distraught over the rising anti-Semitism in Germany under Adolf Hitler. Huberman canceled all his concerts in Germany, refusing to play in a country that would treat Jews with such hatred.

In 1934, Huberman went to Palestine. He was touched by the passion of the people who lived there and was determined to create a symphony orchestra in that country and fill it with Jewish musicians from across Europe who were being discriminated against. He traveled through Czechoslovakia, Austria, Poland, and Hungary to audition these musicians, turning his back to them while they played, and making his decision on who to accept based solely on their musical talent. It was often painful to choose among those who were good enough for this new orchestra and those who were simply not up to the task.

Even though it was virtually impossible for Jews to leave their home countries at this time, and it was equally impossible to find countries that would be willing to take them in, Huberman was able to secure travel documents for his chosen musicians, which enabled them to come to live in Palestine and be part of his new symphony orchestra. At one point, all their travel documents were placed on hold when unrest in Palestine escalated. It took several months before the travel restrictions were lifted and these musicians could finally leave their troubled countries. But not everyone adjusted to life in Palestine. Several of the musicians in Huberman's orchestra decided to leave and return to their home countries. Those musicians and their families were eventually arrested and perished in the death camps that became the horrifying symbol of the Holocaust.

The inaugural concert of the Palestine Symphony Orchestra took place on December 26, 1936. Huberman had even convinced the most famous conductor of that time, Arturo Toscanini, to conduct this opening concert. The concert was attended by two thousand people, including many dignitaries from across Palestine. There were tens of thousands who gathered outside the newly finished concert hall to try to hear a bit of the program. The concert was also broadcast worldwide.

Huberman sat in the audience for that inaugural concert. It is also true that his violin was stolen when he was on tour in the United States. The violin finally surfaced in 1985, long after Huberman's death. In 2001, it was purchased by the American violinist Joshua Bell for a reported four million dollars.

The Palestine Symphony Orchestra went on to become a huge success, and in 1948, they played at the formation of the state of Israel and were renamed the Israeli Philharmonic Orchestra. They continue to play to this day. Many famous musicians have played with the Israeli Philharmonic Orchestra. And over the years, several of the descendants of the original Huberman orchestra have gone on to play in the Israeli Philharmonic. The current conductor, Zubin Mehta, will retire in 2018.

There were approximately seventy Jewish musicians

who were part of the original orchestra that Bronislaw Huberman created. But he also managed to get travel documents for the families of those musicians. In all, he brought approximately one thousand Jewish people to Palestine between 1935 and 1939. He saved all of their lives and the generations that would follow them.

Sources

1. *Hitler: The Pathology of Evil*, G. Victor, Potomac Books, 2008, p. 92
2. http://www.pbs.org/wnet/orchestra-of-exiles/star-violinist-who-saved-jews-before-the-holocaust/